MAN OF LAW

by the same author

THE HARD HIT
DEATH OF A BIG MAN
LANDSCAPE WITH VIOLENCE
ACQUITTAL
WHO GOES NEXT?
THE BASTARD
POOL OF TEARS
A NEST OF RATS
DO NOTHIN' TILL YOU HEAR FROM ME
THE JURY PEOPLE
THIEF OF TIME
A RIPPLE OF MURDERS
BRAINWASH
DUTY ELSEWHERE
THE EYE OF THE BEHOLDER
THE VENUS FLY-TRAP
DOMINOES

MAN OF LAW

John Wainwright

ST. MARTIN'S PRESS • NEW YORK

Copyright © 1980 by John and Avis Wainwright
For information, write: St. Martin's Press,
175 Fifth Avenue, New York, N.Y. 10010
Manufactured in the United States of America

Library of Congress Cataloging in Publication Data

Wainwright, John William, 1921-
        Man of law.

        I.   Title.
PR6073.A354M36   1981   823'.914   80-53086
ISBN 0-312-51088-8

PRE-TRIAL

ONE

'And the old libido? How's that functioning these days?'

And, when asked a question like that, how does a man respond? Or, to be precise, how does a man respond when the question is asked by somebody like Martin Webb? To his friends, 'Marty'. To the academic world, Dr Martin Webb, Professor of Psychology and Criminal Psychiatry at Lessford University; author of *Quirks of the Criminal Mind, Penal Psychology, Psychiatry and Modern Crime*... and a handful of lesser known works. But, to those who knew him – to his legion of friends – the same old Marty.

We'd first met in the salad days of slightly mad undergraduateship; he was a member of the medical faculty, I (of course) was in the law faculty. Our original point of contact had been a mutual fanaticism for traditional jazz. Much as present-day youth raves about the electronic sounds produced by modern heroes of cacophony we in our time (and with equal fervour) had lauded the small-group combinations beloved of three decades ago. The Benny Goodman Trio and Quartet. Eddie Condon and his Chicagoans. Red Nichols and his Five Pennies. The Quintet of The Hot Club of France. Dozens – scores – of small groups, some long forgotten, some still as popular as ever; each (to us) with its own style and its own magic.

Then, after the frantic scramble of all-night crammings, we'd scraped through the Finals and (miraculously) Marty had been pronounced a more-or-less

7

qualified medical practitioner, and I'd become an 'academic lawyer'.

For myself I'd been accepted as pupil in one of the established Gray's Inn chambers. I'd 'dined' the required number of times, passed the not-too-difficult exam and, after the obligatory three years, had been 'called'. I was a barrister and, as a junior, had been fortunate enough to stay on at those same chambers. Gradually, I'd taken Criminal Law as my speciality . . . more often than not defending. With experience had come some success. I'd been duly presented with my red bag to replace my previous blue one and, some years ago, had applied to the Lord Chancellor and 'taken silk'.

Marty, in a manner of speaking, had taken a contradistinctive route. Contradistinctive and, it must be admitted, more successful. At a time when psychology had been a groping forward into darkness, through a door unlocked by Freud and his contemporaries – when psychiatry was viewed as little more than parlour-trickery – Marty had chosen to concentrate upon the medical discipline which concerns itself with the mind. Having won his Ph.D in psychology he had first concentrated upon hospital work then, gradually, he had widened his field and at various times had worked with, and under, some of the great pioneers of the Western world; men like Yellowlees, Eysenck and Stafford-Clark. For a few years he'd been Reader and Lecturer at one of the Redbrick Universities then, when the Chair of Psychology and Criminal Psychiatry had been created at Lessford University, his appointment as its first professor had been almost a foregone conclusion.

Then, gradually, he'd become known as *the* expert on criminal mentality. Whenever a plea of Insanity, or even Diminished Responsibility, had seemed a likely move on the part of the Defence, Marty had been called as a Crown witness . . . and so often he'd cut the ground

8

from under such a plea before it could even be made. The popular press had dubbed him 'The Spilsbury of The Mind' and that, I suppose, summed up his stature in any court of law. Virtually unchallengeable within his own field. But never condescending, always fair and ever ready to say whatever could be said in favour of the accused.

Oddly enough, we'd never lost touch with each other. Our original undergraduate friendship had been stronger than either of us had supposed; our letters to each other, although at times spasmodic, had never tapered off into complete silence and, whenever he'd visited the capital, we'd enjoyed an evening's relaxation, bringing ourselves up to date and reminiscing about the old days at university.

And now this . . .

For the first time in my career, I was defending in a Crown Court of the North Eastern Circuit. Lessford Crown Court. The case was one of murder, I was leading for the Defence, and Marty was one of the main Prosecution witnesses – the Prosecution's main expert witness – and we were dining together on the Saturday evening, prior to the case being opened on the Monday.

In strict fact (and, if this story is to mean anything, it must be factually accurate) we'd already *dined* – a first-class meal at a particularly fine restaurant – and by silent but mutual consent had left the gentle background chatter of the dining room and, carrying our coffee and brandy, had sought the privacy of a small and deserted lounge. We'd settled ourselves in deep and comfortable armchairs, and Marty had produced the only thing missing . . . two superb cigars.

And as he leaned forward and allowed me to roll the end of my cigar in the flame of his lighter, he grinned and said, 'And the old libido? How's that functioning these days?'

I turned the end of my cigar in the flame for a moment

longer than was necessary, as I contemplated possible answers to the question.

Then I side-stepped the question by saying, 'A subject of only comparative importance, I fear.'

'Really?' His eyes twinkled, as he held the end of his own cigar in the flame.

'The price of a developed maturity,' I murmured.

'We once called it old age and poverty.' The twinkle became a smile.

'We were once younger.'

'True . . . even yesterday.' He closed the lighter, and returned it to his pocket. 'But – surely? – you don't yet consider yourself old.'

'Middle-aged.' I tasted good cigar smoke. 'In a few years' time I'll admit to being elderly.'

'The profession.'

'Possibly,' I admitted. 'It tends towards mustiness.'

'Mine doesn't.' He allowed blue-grey smoke to trickle from his nostrils. 'I'm a child. All of us . . . we're still children, playing with dynamite.'

I moved my shoulders.

He went on, 'And the young Turks with whom we argue, those we supposedly teach, they keep us young.'

'Whereas the Bar is no place for Turks, young or old.'

There was a lull in our talk; one of those conversational pauses which, when friends meet and chat, is more of a verbal punctuation mark than a silence. We smoked cigars, we sipped coffee, we tasted good brandy and, as unobtrusively as possible, I watched this old and valued friend of mine.

He was, I knew, a squash enthusiast and the game kept him superbly fit. Like me he was within easy reach of the fifty mark, but he carried not an ounce of superfluous fat; indeed, and without much effort, one could imagine the young ladies of his lecture rooms suffering what were once called 'schoolgirl crushes' on this lean, bronzed, silver-haired man who still had a bounce to his step and who enjoyed a personal charisma of such rarity as to be almost unique.

On reflection, it ever was so. In our undergraduate days *he* had always been the leader. To enjoy his friendship had been a form of accolade, and yet the simple honesty of the man – his basic decency – had prevented any of those friendships from being shallow. He was a rare breed. A man upon whom the ladies fawned . . . and yet a man's man. I could name women who had adored him. I could name no man who had ever disliked him.

He leaned back in his chair and murmured, 'Patsold.'

'Should we?' I felt a slight unease at the turn of the conversation.

'Originally,' he mused, 'a German name, I think. Patzold spelt with a *z*. Anglicised, Patsold spelt with an *s*. Not German. English. Very English. His practice was in Pendlebridge.'

'Should we?' I repeated gently.

In the past when he'd been required as witness at the Central Criminal Court, or at courts on the Oxford and Western Circuits, I'd wined and dined him at my club. Twice (once as a junior, once as a leader) I'd been defending while he'd been a witness for the Prosecution. It had made no difference. Our regard for each other had not suffered and (by what I'd accepted as normal convention) our talk had excluded even passing mention of the cases yet to be heard.

But now . . .

He lowered his head, leaned forward in his chair and said, 'Yes . . . we *should*.'

'The matter *is* sub judice,' I reminded him.

'Between friends? In private?'

'In the circumstances, rather more than friends,' I smiled.

'Point taken.' He carefully rolled the first cylinder of white ash from his cigar into a heavy glass ash-tray on

11

the small table alongside his chair. The impression was that he was concentrating upon not ruining the symmetry of the glowing tobacco leaf as he continued, 'Nevertheless, you're here because I suggested you as Defence counsel . . . *to* Patsold. Personally. I know him. As an acquaintance. I respect him as an above-average medical practitioner interested – very interested – in psychology.' The ash rolled free. He turned, looked at me and said, 'We're both on the same side, Simon, in effect. The side of the truth.'

I played for time. I said, 'I didn't know that.'

'What?'

'That I'm here because of your recommendation.'

'I wanted him to have a good lawyer.'

I moved my head in polite acknowledgement of the implied compliment.

Marty said, 'You'll be seeing the solicitor?'

'Armstrong? Yes, I've arranged to see him at . . .'

'He can't tell you all the truth. I can.'

'Marty . . .' I moved the hand holding the cigar. 'I hardly need remind you. Within a few days you'll be in a witness box. I'll be defending Patsold. There's a chance – every chance – that I'll be cross-examining you. Assuming we ignore the sub judice argument. Assuming you're right . . . that between friends and in private the sub judice argument doesn't exist. You may regret whatever it is you feel you'd like to tell me.'

'I won't regret it.'

'Very well.' I continued to move the hand holding the cigar. 'But what about Clipstone? He mightn't . . .'

'Clipstone's a Q.C. Like you.'

'*Not* like me. He's prosecuting.'

'He's a Q.C. He's an honourable man. Like you – like me – he's seeking the truth.'

'He's presenting a case.'

'He's already *presented* the case at the lower court. Dammit, Simon, I know the rules of this game. You've

12

read the depositions. You know what every prosecution witness is likely to say.'

'Not your evidence, Marty,' I said solemnly. 'Because I wasn't called at the magistrate's hearing.'

'Therefore . . .'

'Therefore in two days' – three days' – time you'll hear, under oath, what I'm going to tell you now. You'll cross-examine me. More bits and pieces might come out . . . but only *might*. Out there in the Crown Court we'll both be hemmed in by rules of evidence. By personal whims of a judge. What is it? "Justice will manifestly be *seen* to be done." A nice phrase, Simon. But it means damn-all. Because we're talking about a man's mind. A sickness you can't X-ray. A thought process almost beyond explanation . . . and certainly beyond any evidence admissible in a court of law.'

'Marty,' I sighed, 'I'm not questioning your motive.'

'Then listen.' He finished his brandy at a gulp and placed the empty glass, alongside his coffee, on the table. 'That's all I ask . . . just listen.'

All my professional life I had lived with lawyers; barristers, solicitors, clerks, even judges; in chambers, in court, at the club, at chosen eating houses and drinking spots within easy distance of the various Inns. Some might have counted it a very sheltered life, but they would have been wrong. Lawyers love to talk shop – to gossip, if you like – and there is no perversion, and no evil, which has not at some time come to the notice of some lawyer and, thereafter, been a subject of conversation and sometimes heated argument. We (the lawyers) are but one step removed from those we prosecute and defend. We are all, at one time or another, 'approached'; the criminal fraternity are ever anxious to use us; very often witnesses are there for the asking . . . and the buying. And every time an attempt is made to nudge justice from its true course, that attempt is broadcast within the legal world. This forensic 'open diplomacy'

13

is, perhaps, one reason why these 'approaches' rarely come to anything. We have a pride – a code of conduct – of which we are almost childishly jealous.

What I'm getting at is this . . .

In all my years at the Bar I had never heard of a responsible witness for the Prosecution – and, even more than that, the main medical witness for the Prosecution – insist that the Q.C. defending listen to pre-trial evidence. Not merely offer to tell, you understand, but insist that he be heard.

Had it been anybody but Marty I think I would have stood up and walked away. As it was, I remained there. I listened (because I could not but hear) and, as a sop to my conscience, I promised myself *not* to use what I was about to be told – other, that is, than what came out in court – either in cross-examination or summing-up.

Marty could talk. He could lecture. His story, therefore, was both coherent and without undue dramatics. Nevertheless, his voice – a beautiful voice, the voice of an actor – left no doubt as to the depth of his feeling.

He said, 'We have to start a few years back. At Pendlebridge. A detective sergeant – a chap called Bowling – killed his daughter, a "mercy killing" if ever there was one.* Jerry – Jerry Patsold – was Bowling's doctor. He was also Mrs Bowling's doctor. Kate Bowling. A good doctor, make no mistake about that. A good doctor with a patient whose husband had turned from detective sergeant to murderer – to the murderer of their only child – and who had to be helped to live with that experience.

'Wisdom after the event. Patsold should have referred Kate Bowling to a specialist. To me, perhaps. To somebody more knowledgeable about the workings of a crippled mind than a general practitioner. He didn't. Understand me, Simon, I'm not criticising him. For

Home Is the Hunter by John Wainwright, Macmillan, 1979.

what he was – a G.P. – he did a damn good job. He pulled her through. Slowly – gently – he steadied her. But it took years, and it took a lot of work, and it took a lot of patience. It also took love. Not love of Kate Bowling personally. Not that sort of individual love. But a more general love. A love of calling, if you like. A love of humanity. Something Jerry Patsold had – still has – in abundance, but something which has a backlash.'

Marty paused in his story. He moistened his lips with coffee, returned the cup to the table, drew reflectively on the cigar, then leaned back in his armchair.

He continued, 'The picture then. Jerry Patsold. A conscientious medic. An overworked G.P. in a market town. And, in addition, the Kate Bowling thing.

'This love aspect. This love of humanity I was talking about. Necessary. *Very* necessary. But every working psychologist – every working psychiatrist – knows all about the backlash and takes what precautions he can. If the patient is of the opposite sex, that love becomes a very personal thing. It's wrongly identified, and it's returned.

'Bear that in mind, Simon. Look at things from Kate Bowling's point of view. Her whole life crumbles around her ears . . . *and* in a tiny market town where tittle-tattle is the order of the day. She seeks help from her G.P. . . . who also, incidentally, happens to be her friend. Her 'G.P. – Patsold – does a good job. Gives her a shoulder to cry on. Comforts her. Props her up and returns her to more-or-less normality. Now, the fact is, she's not cured – not *quite* cured – but she *thinks* she is. That's the state of her mind. And in that state of mind she's convinced that this man – this god, who's lifted her out of hell itself – is in love with her; she's *personalised* that universal love of mankind necessary before any medical man could have even started to help her. And, what's more, she *thinks* she's in love with him. Dammit, she *is* in love with him . . . in her own way. Puppy-love. Infatuation. A very vital part of her own recovery. But she's unable to recognise it as such.' He sighed, then said, 'God, the number of times *that's* happened!'

I now knew why Marty had reached such pre-eminence in his profession. He told it so simply. So succinctly. With a lesser man what he had already explained would have required a full chapter in some ponderous textbook; a bespattering of pompous 'terms of art' would have side-tracked the reader (or the listener) away from the all-important thread of truth. I felt that I already knew the unhappy Kate Bowling. That I already knew my equally unhappy client, Gerald Patsold. I relaxed in my armchair, smoked my cigar, sipped coffee and brandy . . . and listened without interrupting.

Marty continued, 'That was the situation, oh, about a year ago. It's still the situation today. But about a year ago Jerry enrolled as an extra-mural student in some evening classes we ran from the university. *The Psychology of Twentieth-Century Stress.* God knows how he found the time . . . he must have averaged about four hours of sleep a night. That's how I came to know him. That's how I came to know the story of Kate Bowling.

'In the main we run these courses of external lectures as an encouragement to self-education. Occasionally – very occasionally – we net somebody like Jerry. A professional man anxious to learn more about some aspect of his profession. When such a student *is* enrolled we count it a bonus . . . and, I suppose, tend to give him or her preferential treatment. We did with Jerry. After the first couple of classes I got into the habit of taking him for a drink at the university club after the class had broken up. Two professional men – like you and me – talking shop together. He asked for advice. I gave it . . . willingly. Whether he took it or not . . .' Marty shrugged.

He drew on the cigar, tasted the coffee, then continued, 'What I expected to happen *did* happen. He flaked out

16

part-way through one of the classes. Nothing too serious. Just over-work. But I drove him home and met his wife, Beth.'

Marty paused. We were, I knew, approaching the thin ice. Up to that moment what he'd told me was interesting – even instructive – but, by the strict rules of evidence, not *res gestae*. A liberal judge *might* have allowed mention of what I now knew in a summing-up plea . . . but, if so, only passing mention. And, even so, he would have had to be a *very* liberal judge. But now the victim – Elizabeth Patsold – had been introduced into the story to take her place alongside her husband, the murderer. The pace of Marty's talk slowed a little. I think he chose his words – indeed, his mode of telling – with infinite care.

'General practitioners,' he mused gently. 'The wives of general practitioners. Ever noticed, Simon? Very often they're nurses. Apart from the fact that young medics and young nurses get thrown together on the wards I sometimes think there's another reason. A sort of subconscious acceptance on the part of the man that the odds in favour of a happy marriage are increased if the woman has first-hand knowledge of what she's letting herself in for. Whatever . . .' He spread his palms. 'They're letting themselves in for something. The wives, I mean.

'Beth Patsold *wasn't* a nurse. Daughter of some nine-till-five local authority employee, which was no grounding at all for being the wife of a small-town medic. Rough hours. Very little social life. A dog-tired husband. She tried – I'm not saying she didn't try – but it was a way of life she couldn't even begin to understand.

'Then along came Kate Bowling. Damn it, it *wasn't* the old "eternal triangle". That's the sad thing about all this. It *wasn't* what Kate Bowling believed it to be. But because Kate Bowling behaved like a moon-struck calf – because Jerry had wisdom enough not to knock her down into the depths again – because he refused to be unkind to her and undo all the good he'd done . . . that's one hell of a motive for murder, Simon. One hell of a motive! But, basically, that *was* the motive.

'Beth couldn't see that. I tried to explain things to her. Damn it . . . I *tried*. I can understand, because I'm trained. Jerry could understand, because he knew enough about the fine balance of an unquiet mind. *You* can understand – I hope – because you're far enough away to be objective, and because you have an imagination. But Beth? Never! She couldn't understand and she wouldn't accept the truth.

'She gave Jerry hell. Kate was "the other woman" . . . and nothing would convince her otherwise. So, what with too much work, the very real problem of Kate's infatuation and Beth's bloody stupid attitude, Jerry was charging, head-down, for a crack-up. I suggested Lentizol – that's the brand name of a good tricyclic antidepressant – and I think he dosed himself with about fifty milligrammes a day . . . a handful of cement thrown at a crack in a dam. Well, one evening the dam burst . . . and you'll find the rest in the depositions.'

TWO

That, then, is how it started. It would be some slight exaggeration to claim that Marty's determination to trample upon the rigid conventions of our respective professions ruined an otherwise pleasant evening. Such is not the case. Having unburdened himself he seemed, figuratively speaking, to close a book; he left the tiny lounge in order to replenish his brandy and when he returned nothing more was said about the pending case or any of the people involved therein.

18

The talk (as always) touched upon our days at university.

And (again as always) my own contribution lacked the sparkle of Marty's reminiscences. Not for the first time I realised what a dull dog I must have seemed. And, by contrast, what a devil-may-care extrovert Marty had been . . . and still was. His talk of conquests was not the talk of a braggart. If necessary, I could vouch for the fact that he had been virtually irresistible.

'I wouldn't call them orgies,' he chuckled. 'Not by today's standards.'

'Not by today's standards,' I agreed.

'But, by God, we had some wild nights.'

I smiled agreement.

'Remember the Pearson girl?'

'The – er – Pearson girl?'

'Alice Pearson. She was in your lot, the Law Faculty.'

'Ah, yes.' I nodded. 'Alice Pearson.'

'Virginity personified.'

'Was she?' I murmured.

'Until we got her sloshed. It was her birthday, I think, something like that.' The chuckle came again. 'She wasn't a virgin after *that*.'

'I – er – I wouldn't know,' I murmured.

'You wouldn't . . .?' He stared, then held his head on one side as he said, 'No. You wouldn't, old son, would you?' There was genuine surprise in his tone. 'Come to think of it. Damnation . . . I hadn't *realised*.'

'You had other friends.'

'True.' The sudden smile was a little lop-sided. 'A lot of friends . . . some of whom turned out to be slightly *un*friendly.'

'If you recall, I was never one for the ladies.'

'True.' He nodded.

'But – again, if you recall – I could drink.'

'Ah, the wine! The booze. The hooch.'

'That first morning of the Finals.' I shook my head

19

in mock-despair. 'The hangover. How I passed remains a mystery.'

'But we did pass, Simon, old son. We *did* pass. By the skin of our teeth . . . agreed. But we've both made up for it since.'

And so it went on. The ping-pong ball of remembrance. How it had once been . . . how it now was. The then and the now. The past and the present. We chuckled, we laughed, we smiled and, occasionally, we frowned at the memory of some moment which, even with the passing of time, retained some degree of hurt.

It was that sort of evening; the sort of evening it had always been, at our spasmodic get-togethers. And, when we parted, we were both ever so slightly drunk.

I took a taxi back to the hotel, arranged with the night porter to have black coffee sent up to my room, then showered and changed into pyjamas and dressing-gown. Then, as I sipped black sobering coffee, I unknotted the scarlet tape on the brief and re-examined the evidence for the defence of Gerald Patsold.

As a result of Marty's story the man was becoming three-dimensional. More – much more – than the name of one more client; much more than a set of carefully tabulated facts to be presented to a jury within the strict limits allowed by the law of evidence.

This realisation worried me a little. As a barrister – as a Q.C. who had earned something of a reputation as a defender – I knew the weakness of involvement. The first rule of success at the Bar – prosecuting or defending – centres around the importance of objectivity. Personal opinions are not merely unnecessary, they can be positively deadly. Crippling at the very least. My job was to plead . . . nothing more. To take a name – in this case the name Gerald Patsold – and, via a solicitor, present to a court whatever version of a set of circumstances that name has conveyed to that solicitor. A good barrister – a successful barrister – is always one remove from his client. Sometimes even two removes; if, as some-times happens, some point requires clarification and the solicitor feels he needs the presence of some third party at his interview with the client . . . that is one of the tasks of the junior barrister, who always works with a Queen's Counsel. One remove. Two removes. But *never* involved.

Nevertheless, I sat on the edge of my bed, I sipped black coffee, I smoked cigarettes, I re-read the brief . . . and I became involved.

It was almost midnight when I lifted the receiver of the bedside telephone, asked the night porter to give me an outside line, then dialled Armstrong's home number.

I freely admit that I had a feeling of guilt. As yet I hadn't even met Armstrong. We'd corresponded. We'd had three (perhaps four) prolonged telephone conversations between Pendlebridge and my chambers. That I knew his home telephone number was entirely due to Armstrong's own insistence. I knew he had a young voice; it seemed, therefore, reasonable to assume that he wasn't one of those parchment-minded solicitors to whom a midnight telephone call might be a form of minor blasphemy. And from the way he'd talked on our previous telephone conversations I hazarded a guess that he knew Patsold personally; that he knew him and liked him.

The speed at which he answered the telephone sug-gested a bedside extension. The yawning quality of his voice left me in no doubt but that I had awakened him from sleep.

He muttered, 'Reg Armstrong.'

I said, 'Whitehouse here.'

'Who?'

'Simon Whitehouse. I'm defending Gerald Patsold at ' . .'

'Oh, yes . . . Mr Whitehouse.' He was suddenly wide awake. 'Sir, don't tell me you can't make the hearing on . . .'

21

'I'm already here. At Lessford.'

I could hear the sigh of relief quite distinctly.

I said, 'Mr Armstrong, forgive me for ringing you up at this unearthly hour . . .'

'That's quite all right, sir.'

'. . . but certain information has come to my know-ledge.'

'About Jerry? About Patsold?'

'About Patsold,' I agreed. 'It – er – it isn't important where I obtained this information, but I would like it verified.'

'Yes, sir. Tonight?'

I must admit that I blinked with surprise at his eagerness. He was (very obviously) prepared to leap from his bed and rush off to do my bidding, regardless of the hour . . . as long as it was likely to help Patsold. It made quite an impression on me. More than that. It seemed to 'involve' me even more with this client of mine.

I said, 'It – er – it might not be convenient, tonight, but . . .'

'It's no trouble, sir.'

'. . . if you know a lady called Bowling. Kate Bowling. I understand her husband was once a detective sergeant . . .'

'I'm sorry. Jack Bowling's dead, sir.'

'Oh!'

'I'm very sorry . . .'

'That's not important, Mr Armstrong,' I interrupted. 'It's his wife I'm interested in.'

'Kate Bowling. I know her well, sir.'

'I'd like to meet her.'

'Certainly. This evening?'

'This – er – this evening?'

'I could ring her. We could be at Lessford in less than an hour from now.'

'Good Lord!'

'Sir?'

'You have a very loose definition of "evening", Mr Armstrong.'

Somehow I knew he was smiling as he said, 'I'm sorry, sir.'

'Don't apologise for enthusiasm. There's little enough of it about.'

'It's not just enthusiasm.' And with equal certainty I knew he was no longer smiling. 'I like Jerry Patsold. We're very good friends.'

'And his wife?' I ventured.

'I – I liked her, too.' But the tone of his voice suggested certain qualifications.

I said, 'For herself? Or because she was Patsold's wife?'

'Sir . . .' He hesitated, then blurted, 'You're at Lessford?'

'Yes.'

'Not in bed, are you?'

'Not yet,' I admitted with absolute truth.

Again there was hesitation before he said, 'Could I come across?'

'To Lessford?'

'Would it be too inconvenient?'

'Now? At this hour?'

'I could be there in no time at all.'

'Mr Armstrong,' I said slowly, 'I detect an uncommon amount of urgency in your voice.'

'It *is* urgent, Mr Whitehouse. Very urgent.'

'Indeed?'

In a voice which carried absolute conviction he said, 'He's not guilty, sir.'

'As you know, we intend pleading . . .'

'I'm not talking about the plea. I'm not talking law. I'm talking facts. *Jerry Patsold didn't kill his wife.*'

THREE

My colleagues at Gray's Inn would, no doubt, have considered me mad. Indeed, I myself would have been hard pressed to argue any real degree of sanity. Membership of the Bar presupposes a very pedestrian attitude of mind; one does not jump to conclusions; one is not press-ganged into wild and unsubstantiated propositions to be discussed in the small hours of the morning.

It was (I told myself) Marty's fault. Marty and his infernal refusal to allow the law to take its proper course. Marty and his never-ending urge to do things 'his way' . . . however stupid and wrong 'his way' might be.

I recall (having contacted the long-suffering night porter and arranged for more coffee and sandwiches to be brought to my room) muttering to myself, 'Marty, you're a damn nuisance. Will I *ever* get you out of my system?'

Meanwhile . . .

I felt a little foolish. I was a Q.C. and men and women of that exalted position are neither required nor expected to meet young and gushing solicitors in hotel bedrooms in the small hours of the morning . . . and clad only in pyjamas and dressing-gown! The situation was something thought up by some over-imaginative Hollywood script writer. Ridiculous, but it was happening. Indeed, I was reminded of the fiction of my youth; of the stories of the excellent and prolific American writer Erle Stanley Gardner and his entertaining (but quite outrageous) character, Perry Mason. I had once enjoyed – one might even say 'devoured' – the forensic adventures of the fictitious Mr Mason but, as the realities of workaday criminal law had been brought home to me, I had become . . .

Oh, no! Not a 'real life' Perry Mason. The thought, when it struck me, terrified me. Frenzied pre-case activity was for writers of fiction. Court-room confrontations were for the purveyors of exaggerated forensic drama. In real life . . .

Unfortunately, in real life (or to be precise at that moment in *my* real life) middle-aged barristers, dressed in their night attire, waited in hotel bedrooms at impossible hours for the arrival of unknown, but over-enthusiastic solicitors in order to discuss strange aspects of a murder case.

And that (I was forced to concede) was *not* fiction.

Armstrong arrived at a few minutes before one o'clock, and he was exactly what I had feared he would be. Young; not more than four years past thirty at a guess. He was slim, fit and ridiculously awake and alert for the hour. His suit was of a lightweight, medium grey material, under which he wore a dark blue, poplin shirt. Instead of a tie he wore a silk scarf, tied cravat-fashion. He was, in short, a very presentable young man; at that moment, far more presentable than I, in that he had obviously taken time to run an electric razor over the skin of his face in order to remove the inevitable 'shadow' which I knew gave my own features that vaguely unwashed appearance.

I welcomed him into the bedroom, took his document case and placed it on the bed, settled him into a chair, offered him coffee and sandwiches (which he accepted with a grateful smile) then asked the question to which I required an answer.

'Mr Armstrong, what makes you so sure Patsold didn't kill his wife?'

25

'Sir, I know the man.'

I compressed my lips and looked disappointed.

'I've known him all my life. I've known his wife all my life. He didn't kill her.'

'And that,' I sighed, 'from a qualified lawyer.'

'Mr Whitehouse . . .' he began.

'Mr Armstrong,' I interrupted. I buried my hands in the pockets of my dressing-gown and walked to the window of the bedroom. The curtains had not been closed and, from two floors above ground level, I stared out at the deserted side-streets and yards of Lessford. It was a dismal, uninspiring scene; high, goose-necked standards from which orange-coloured flood-lighting seemed to accentuate the shadows, rather than illuminate the road surface; what seemed to be acres of dark, slated roofs; a sky, moonless and without stars; in the far distance a glow which suggested the illumination of marshalling yards. A city, like a thousand other cities. A case, like a thousand other cases . . . and yet it refused to *be* like a thousand other cases. Therefore I interrupted and said, 'Mr Armstrong, I travelled north for the purpose of defending Patsold. Nothing less, but at the same time nothing more. It was my intention – it is *still* my intention – of entering a plea of Diminished Responsibility. Having read the brief, that was my advice. I communicated that advice to you. You in turn – presumably – communicated that advice to Patsold. Patsold decided to accept that advice. The whole case has, until this moment, rested upon . . .'

From behind me Armstrong said, 'Against *my* advice, sir.'

'I beg your pardon?'

'He accepted *your* advice, against *my* advice. *I* advised him to plead Not Guilty.'

I breathed heavily and continued to stare out of the window. There was little worth looking at but against the semi-reflective pane I could see Armstrong watching the nape of my neck. His expression was, at once, both interesting and pathetic; a perfect mix of trepidation and bloody-mindedness.

He said, 'At the committal hearing I pleaded Not Guilty.'

'A formality.'

'Not . . .' I saw him moisten his lips. 'Not as far as *I* was concerned.'

'Mr Armstrong.' I turned slowly from the window. I spoke as quietly and as calmly as possible. I said, 'Mr Armstrong . . . forgive me. But if Patsold, in effect, insists that he killed his wife, how the devil can you insist that he *didn't*?'

'He's copping out.'

'I don't understand. I . . .'

'That means . . .'

'Damn it, Armstrong, I know what the expression "copping out" means. I may live a sheltered life, but that does not, necessarily, equate with being packed away in a cardboard carton when not in use.'

'I'm sorry, sir.'

'What I do *not* understand is why a man should agree to plead guilty when he's innocent. That's not copping out. That's being mad.'

'He's had enough,' muttered Armstrong.

'And does he seriously think a term in prison won't give him more?'

'He's – he's lost the will to fight.'

'Oh, my God!' I flapped my elbows. Had I removed my hands from the pockets of my dressing-gown, I might have thrown them high in disgust. As it was, I flapped my elbows. I moved to the bed, sat down and said, 'You've read the depositions, presumably?'

'Yes.'

'The police are liars?' I said sarcastically.

'No, sir.'

'The police are *not* liars?'

27

'They're not liars, sir. I know the detective inspector on the case. He's not a liar.'

'The forensic scientists are liars?'

'No, sir. That's absurd.'

'Something's absurd,' I agreed coldly. 'The forensic scientist gave evidence at the lower court. Patsold's wife died from manual strangulation . . . am I right so far?'

'Yes, sir.'

'Violent manual strangulation. So violent, indeed, that the nails of her killer gouged into the flesh of her neck?'

'That was the evidence.'

'You're disputing that evidence?'

'No, sir.'

'Thank heaven for small mercies. But to return to the evidence. The victim fought back . . . naturally. She clawed the face of her assailant.'

'It would seem so.'

'It would only *seem* so?'

'I'll accept the evidence,' he muttered.

'Magnanimous of you. Will you also accept the sworn testimony that Patsold was badly scratched about the face?

'I saw the scratches myself. They were bad.'

'That a microscopic examination of the victim's nail-parings revealed tiny particles of flesh from Patsold's face?'

'I've no option. I have to accept that.'

'That further microscopic examination, this time of nail parings taken from Patsold, revealed particles of flesh also . . . from the neck of his wife?'

'I know. I know.' He sounded desperate.

'And that not once – not *once* – has Patsold denied strangling his wife to death.'

'Nor has he admitted it.'

'Copping out – your own expression – saying neither yea nor nay?'

'Walking away from it. Allowing the world to spin on its own bloody axis . . . without *his* help.'

'Mr Armstrong.' I tilted my head and stared at the ceiling. 'How many murder cases have you handled?'

'This is my second,' he admitted. 'The first was Bowling . . . when he killed his daughter.'

'Ah, Bowling,' I murmured.

'I liked him, too.'

'I *don't* like murderers,' I murmured. 'As a class I find them either boring or unfriendly. And I've met more than a few.'

'And defended most of them.'

I nodded agreement at the ceiling.

'Therefore why not defend Jerry?'

'Diminished Responsibility . . . that *is* a defence.'

'Not Guilty. That's his *real* defence.' Before I could answer he continued, 'We try to prove he's half mad in the hope of a reduction – murder to manslaughter – and a lesser sentence. The Prosecution guess our move – our very *obvious* move – and allow us to do some of their work for them. They push the madness thing just that little farther. Bring evidence to suggest that he's *really* round the twist . . . work for a Guilty but Insane verdict. That way he gets an open-ended sentence. Detained, pending Her Majesty's pleasure. And he ends up with a longer sentence than he'd have caught had he pleaded Guilty in the first place.'

I lowered my eyes, glared at him a little, and said, 'You're suggesting certain wheeling and dealing.'

'No.'

'The Prosecution are out for the truth . . . no more.'

'The Prosecution,' he said tightly, 'are out for a conviction. It's their job. It's their duty. They already have their big guns lined up. Webb . . . that's what *he's* there for.'

I leaned forward, took a cigarette from a packet on

the bedside table and lighted it. While I smoked, Armstrong allowed me silence in which to think. Armstrong sipped at his coffee and nibbled his way through one of the sandwiches. From somewhere along the hotel corridor a door opened then closed. A clock – some town clock, away in the distance – struck the half-hour.

Having partly smoked the cigarette, I squashed it out in an ash-tray alongside the packet, then said, 'If we change the plea at this point . . .'

I didn't end the sentence.

'We don't have to change the plea. I pleaded Not Guilty at the lower court.'

'Tactics,' I growled.

'They're expecting a Diminished Responsibility argument.'

'Obviously. That's why Professor Webb's being called.'

'They'll get a surprise.' He grinned.

'Somebody will.'

'He's innocent, sir. Believe me . . . he's *innocent*.'

'It's a great pity you and eleven more of his friends aren't on the jury.'

The remark removed the grin from his face.

I said, 'I'll need Patsold's blessing before I change the plea.'

'It's yours.'

'From *him*.'

'Yes, sir. But take my word.'

I leaned forward, cupped my chin in one hand, then said, 'We need to alter our plan of attack.'

'Yes, sir.'

'So, let's assume he didn't strangle his wife.'

'He didn't. I'll stake my . . .'

'Let's *assume* he didn't.'

'Yes, sir.'

'But he was there.'

'His own home.'

30

'More than that. He was in the room with the murdered woman.'

'Possibly.'

'*Possibly!*' I felt a rising anger at this young man's refusal to face known facts. 'He was *there*. In the room with the murdered woman. He was found there by his son.'

'By Edward . . . his son.'

I eyed him suspiciously, then said, 'Your tone says more than the words.'

'There's no proof,' he said, moodily.

'Proof?'

'About Edward.'

'Damnation, man,' I exploded, 'there's no proof your precious friend isn't a murderer, but you accept *that* without hesitation. We either deal in proof or we deal in speculation. But if in one, in all. Edward Patsold. My brief insists that he found the newly strangled body of his mother. And in the same room he found his father. True? Or untrue?'

'True.'

'In that case . . .'

'But Edward Patsold takes dope. Hard dope.'

'Does he, by God!' I breathed.

'I'm not saying he was on a trip when he found the . . .'

'Convictions?' I snapped.

'No convictions . . . he's been arrested once and I defended him.'

'You got him off?'

'A pure technicality. He was as guilty as sin.'

'That,' I said, 'must have increased your popularity with the police.'

'The hell with the police.'

'I wish it was as easy as that, my young friend.' As I reached for another cigarette I said, 'Tell me about Edward Patsold.'

'The usual.' He sighed heavily. 'A doctor's son. Jerry

31

wasn't as security conscious as he might have been where dangerous drugs were concerned. Edward helped himself a couple of times. The old, old story. Try it for kicks – it can't happen to you, but it always does. Added to which, he ran around with the wrong crowd.'

'What sort of drugs?' I asked.

'Heroin.'

'And no mention made? In the depositions. The person finding the body and . . .'

'Jerry had him cured. Quietly. A private clinic.'

'Cured?' If disbelief was in the tone of the question, it was because I'd seen so many addicts who'd been 'cured'.

'Are they ever?' Armstrong was no fool.

'Sometimes,' I conceded. 'But not often.'

Armstrong said, 'I think he's back on it. Was back on it when he found the body.'

'You mean under the influence? At that time?'

'No.' The impression was that he would have enjoyed giving an affirmative answer to my question. He added, 'But on that stuff, main-lining – and I think he *was* main-lining – they're never completely clear-headed.'

I smoked meditatively for a moment, then said, 'The picture, then. Edward, the son, discovers his father in the same room as his strangled mother. That . . . plus the scientific evidence covering the nail parings. And you still think we've some sort of chance with a Not Guilty plea?'

'I've already told you. Jerry didn't . . .'

'You've told me. Now convince me.'

'Jerry would have admitted it.'

'He hasn't specifically denied it. I'm not convinced.'

'He was . . .' Armstrong moved his hands.

'What?'

'Not himself.'

'That means nothing.'

'He'd been working hard.'

'*I* work hard. I don't strangle people as a form of relaxation.'

'Hell's bells! I thought you'd decided . . .'

'The questions that are going to be asked by the Prosecution, Armstrong. We can't duck those questions. If they have answers, we have to find them . . . and we haven't much time.'

FOUR

My colleagues – the men and women with whom I spend the greater part of my waking life – would have poured scorn upon my implied decision. Indeed, such was the self-shame that I could not bring myself openly to admit that (subject to Patsold's agreement) a Not Guilty plea was to be substituted for the Diminished Responsibility defence.

My excuse? . . . such as it is.

Armstrong's absolute certainty. His infernal passion. In the course of a not-unsuccessful career I had met many solicitors. Dozens. Scores. Perhaps even hundreds. Some I had liked, some I had disliked, but the majority had been merely conduits via which I received briefs handed to me by the clerk of chambers. They had been names to place alongside the names of clients; names – synonymous with legal arguments – from whom I had received instructions. The jealousy with which the Bar upheld its ancient position, within the forensic hierarchy, insisted that they call me 'sir', but the truth is many of them had been much more learned in law than I. And perhaps that, too, was a factor in my succumbing to Armstrong's enthusiasm. As a barrister – even as a Q.C. – I had learned never lightly to dismiss the opinion of any solicitor. A working solicitor is the P.B.I. of the legal world. He (along with policemen) makes the law work – especially the Criminal Law: they take an Act of Parliament, or a case decision, and from a rigmarole of seemingly contradictory phrases create a more-or-less immaculate two-and-two equation. Indeed, without the High Street solicitor, the bulk of law – *all* law – would remain theoretical nonsense.

Nevertheless . . .

'You have,' I complained, 'presented me with a somewhat difficult dilemma.'

'I'm sorry, sir.' Perhaps the contrition was genuine, but I thought not.

'The day after tomorrow . . .' I glanced at my watch, then corrected myself. 'No – *tomorrow* – Patsold will stand in the dock. He will plead Not Guilty. And, moreover, will *mean* it.'

'We'll fight them.'

'Armstrong . . . for God's sake!' I exploded. In a quieter, but tight tone, I said, 'This isn't a *fight*, Armstrong. In effect, I've been presented with an eleventh-hour change of plea. I'm accepting it. But I'm not liking it . . . and, if it's of any interest to you, I don't really *believe* it. But if – as you say – Patsold verifies this change, so be it. If we can swing the jury into believing him innocent, he'll be a very lucky man. Luckier than he deserves to be. But if we fail – and, personally, I think we *will* fail – he can thank *you* for a longer sentence than he'd have received, had we pleaded Diminished Responsibility.'

FIVE

It was three o'clock – a few minutes after three o'clock – before Armstrong left. Even *he* looked tired. For myself, I felt as though I had not slept for a week. Possibilities. Probabilities. Improbabilities. We'd touched upon them all. In effect, we'd dismembered Patsold, cell at a time, in order to ascertain the *exact* sort of man he was. Armstrong had claimed to have known when he arrived. He still claimed to know when he left. I remained undecided.

The cold logic of a legal training insisted that he *could* be a murderer. He was a man, complete with human strengths and weaknesses, therefore he could murder. Experience left no doubt in my mind as to *that* proposition.

But as counsel for the Defence . . .

Patsold was *not* a murderer. He was innocent. He had *not* killed his wife. I, as defending barrister, was prohibited from having any doubts on the subject. The moment I settled my wig on my head – the moment I pushed my arms into the sleeves of my gown – *from that moment, Patsold was innocent*. Not half-guilty; not guilty with extenuating circumstances; not guilty of manslaughter, but not murder. Innocent . . . of everything!

I climbed into bed and settled down for what little sleep I could tease from the rest of the night. It was useless. The pattern of my life had been broken. I was the very epitome of the old dog quite unable to learn new tricks. With all my heart I yearned for the known and comfortable homeliness of my own flat within easy walking distance of the Victoria and Albert Museum. There I could have taken temporary insomnia in my stride; I could have selected some anthology from my bookshelves, and read myself into a state of drowsiness; I could have mixed myself a stiff drink – perhaps even a hot toddy – without having to make a nuisance of myself to a night porter; I could (in final desperation) have fiddled about with the knobs of my radio and sought out some foreign, all-night station and, with it, some decent soothing music . . . as it was the extension speaker, over my hotel bed, provided modern caterwauling, interspersed by that peculiar brand of non-conversation beloved by so-called disc jockeys, aimed at a mental age of not more than twelve. That or silence . . . and I much preferred the silence.

But silence equated with boredom. And boredom, in turn, brought on increased mental activity . . . and increased mental activity was *not* conducive to sleep.

In desperation, I climbed from bed, re-donned my dressing-gown, pulled the only comfortable chair towards the window, lighted a cigarette and, in the darkness, stared out onto the still-slumbering city and considered the case of Regina versus Patsold.

Know Thine Enemies . . .

Ah, yes. But granting that the word 'enemies' was not too emotive a word, who *were* my enemies?

The police?

Perhaps, but if Armstrong was to be believed, not my mortal enemies. Even Armstrong had refused to be drawn at the suggestion that the police were liars. More. He had specifically asserted that the detective inspector in charge of the case was *not* a liar. But in the past I'd known more than one 'truthful' policeman. Truthful – oh, yes – but until it had been dragged from him, via cross-examination, not *all* the truth.

Accepting Armstrong's assessment at face value, then.

36

The fact remained that policemen did not like 'losing' cases. They fought for convictions. What else? By the very nature of things they had already decided upon the guilt of Patsold; the *absolute* guilt. Anything less, and the charge would not have been made.

The jury?

Twelve good men and true, twelve good women and true, or a rather nasty mix of both. Such a legendary institution. Oh, yes, *they* were my enemy. Every jury which has ever sat at a criminal trial has been the sworn enemy of the Defence. And why? Well – disregarding the halt, the lame, those who wish to get home as soon as possible, the stone deaf, those who are convinced that *all* our policemen are wonderful and those who consider jury service as an infernal nuisance – disregarding those, the few non-numskulls see the accused in the dock and, far from that beloved Presumption of Innocence everlastingly prated about by academic writers of legal tomes, there is an immediate and near-immovable Presumption of *Guilt*. 'He wouldn't be there otherwise.' Thus go their thought-processes, and they may deny this monumental bias until Old Nick serves ice-cream in Hell, but every defending barrister knows the truth of the matter. To raise a doubt – *any* degree of doubt – in the collective mind of a jury is a Herculean task.

There are, of course, tricks; subtleties known to every defending barrister worth his fee. To watch the jury as the Prosecution presents its case; to pick out two – no more than three – members who look moderately intelligent and who, whenever the Prosecution emphasises a major point, frown or look a little worried. These two – these three – are listening. They have a bias (the bias I have already mentioned) but, to their credit, they are trying to overcome that bias. As far as the Defence is concerned *they* are the jury. Those two. Those three. The other members are superfluous . . . they are merely there to fill the jury bench. The trick, then, is to concentrate the Defence upon those two. Those three. To speak to them directly. To convince *them*. Then pray to God that they, in turn, can convince their fellow-jurors when they retire.

But what if there aren't three? Or two? Or even one? In that case justice could, with equal certainty, depend upon the spin of a coin.

The jury, then, had to be counted as an enemy.

And the witnesses?

The police . . . as I've already mentioned. And with them, Edward Patsold. The son of the murdered woman. But equally the son of the accused man. In the event of a preponderance of love for his mother he might prove difficult. In the event of a preponderance of love for his father he would be easy. In the event of a more or less equal love for both parents one should cancel out the other.

But if Armstrong was to be believed, Edward Patsold was a particularly weak weed from the point of view of the Prosecution. A dope addict. So easy! Give me a dope addict in a witness box and, within fifteen minutes, I guarantee to destroy every shred of his story's credibility. Addicts can *never* control their emotions. Goad them, tease them, scorn them, rattle them . . . they will virtually explode. Always! They will shred their own evidence to ribbons via the spite which they hurl back at their tor-mentor. Edward Patsold, then, numerically an 'enemy', but not a very frightening enemy.

The so-called 'expert evidence'? In particular, Marty?

The tactical advantage of the Prosecution was fairly obvious. In the event of a swing in our favour, bring evidence to show madness and aim for a Guilty but Insane verdict. In the event of a swing to *their* favour, prove complete sanity and thus block a back-up plea of Diminished Responsibility. And, moreover, Marty could do it.

Of them all, Marty was my *real* enemy.

His easy – almost carefree – plausibility made him doubly dangerous. Not for Marty high-sounding terms of art. Not for him that grey area between sanity and madness. He talked the language of the textbook then, immediately, translated that language into the language of the man-in-the-street. And if, in the translation, certain nuances were lost or glossed over what of it? Professor Martin Webb topped the tree of his profession. Over the years only a handful of men had dared to climb into a witness box and contradict his evidence ... and they'd all left the witness box looking foolish, and with tarnished reputations.

An enemy, then. But an enemy against whom I could not hope to array any real strength. He had to be broken. Smashed. But not by counter-evidence. Therefore by the law. Medicine versus The Law. That, too, could have been the name of the case.

The judge?

Ah, well, who knew judges? Belmont was slightly unpredictable – but only slightly so – and that, if anything, was a point in my favour. He was neither as radical as Denning nor as grimly dogmatic as Goddard. It depended (or so it was rumoured) upon the state of his stomach; he was said to eat well and drink moderately and, if his digestive juices were working adequately, the judicial quips – the heavy-handed humour of the Bench – punctuated even the most sombre of trials. Therefore, if his mood was good, the trick was to smile ... but not too readily and not too much. To grant him small victory, but to do it with apparent reluctance.

And, finally, Clipstone?

No ... of them all, Clipstone was *not* my enemy. He was to lead for the Prosecution. He would do his job and do it well, but he would do no more than his job. During the recesses we would eat together, drink together and (as always) dip into our respective memories for some moments of legal recollections with which to garnish our conversations. That . . . as always. We were fellow-barristers; brethren of the Bar; friends who, once we had doffed our wigs, were no longer even rivals. Clipstone was *not* my enemy.

I learned many things that night in that hotel bedroom, as I chain-smoked my way towards the time when the grey-tinged, clear-skied dawn washed, like an incoming tide, across the roof-tops of Lessford. I played forensic war games and, in so doing, I became more conscious of weaknesses and strengths. In myself and in others. I planned a campaign around those strengths and weaknesses and, for the first time, truly believed Patsold's innocence. Why? Because it was necessary; vitally necessary. *I* had to believe . . . otherwise I could convince nobody. Non-belief would have been a hidden weakness, and I wanted as few weaknesses as possible.

I finished the cigarette I was smoking, stripped, shaved very carefully, enjoyed a long and luxurious shower, dried myself slowly, in order to kill more time, then dressed with equal leisure.

By this time it was past six o'clock on the morning of Sunday, June 30th and, in view of his youth (and his proven excess of energy and enthusiasm), I had no compunction in telephoning Armstrong and, once more, disturbing his slumber. He seemed in no way annoyed, and was happy to make my suggested arrangements.

Then I took the lift, strolled into a deserted dining room and, by dint of pleading an urgent appointment, succeeded in obtaining a Continental breakfast of warm rolls, butter and fresh coffee.

SIX

Pendlebridge. A most picturesque market town. Probably *too* picturesque; a little too quaint, and unusual to be allowed to slumber peacefully within the folds of the lower Pennines. It can happen. It often does. To my certain knowledge the parish of Alfriston in Sussex has long been far too beautiful for its own good. The tourists – the car-bound gawpers – they, too, seek beauty and, having found it, destroy it by their presence; like a pack following the scent of a fox they track down peace and tranquillity . . . and butcher it.

It had happened at Alfriston. My guess was that it had happened at Pendlebridge. Other guesses included the size of the population; less than three thousand . . . swollen to almost twice that figure during the tourist season.

There was but one main street – a narrow, steeply-sloping thoroughfare – with tiny off-streets and half-hidden courts; with cafés and public houses, souvenir shops and a ridiculously large car park for such a tiny township.

The driver of my taxi had remarked, 'A nice place at this time.'

'Pendlebridge?'

'Mid-July, August . . . that's when you can't move.'

'I see.'

I paid the taxi at the gate leading to Armstrong's garden and, before that vehicle had time to draw away from the kerb, Armstrong was striding down the path to greet me. He looked disgustingly healthy, and outrageously fresh. A badly interrupted night's sleep (it seemed) was nothing to this young man.

Before I could speak, he opened the gate, and said, 'Everything arranged, sir. First stop, Mrs Bowling. She's up and expecting us. Then the police station. I've fixed things with the divisional superintendent. Detective Inspector Leroy will be there . . . to help.'

'Your friend?'

He nodded. 'A good man. A fair-minded man.'

'I hope so.' I stepped beyond the gate and walked alongside him up the drive. I said, 'Edward Patsold?'

'This afternoon. After lunch.' He glanced at me and added, 'I've fixed lunch, sir. Ruth, my wife, we'd be honoured to provide lunch here, unless . . .'

'Don't lickspittle,' I growled. 'I've eaten in some dumps in my time. Tell your wife. Thank her. *I'd* be honoured.'

'She's a good cook,' he smiled.

'I don't doubt it.' I returned the smile. 'Knowing you – already – if she wasn't when you married her she'd be cordon bleu class before the first year was out.'

He chuckled delightedly and for the first time – and despite the age gap – I had the distinct feeling that we had progressed some way beyond the solicitor/barrister relationship; that we were acquaintances moving smoothly and swiftly towards the status of friends.

We reached a two-car-sized garage, with a green-painted, metal, up-and-over door. Armstrong swung the door upwards and I had my first sight of what I came to realise was one of the loves of this young man's life. I had in the past seen Aston Martins. Not many and for obvious reasons; the Bar and the Bench provide a living, but by the time that living reaches a point where the purchase of such a motor car becomes a viable proposition, age has intervened and a less ostentatious, but no less expensive motor car takes first choice. Which, I suppose, is a pity because an Aston Martin – and in particular *this* Aston Martin – is a very special vehicle ... and makes no effort to hide that fact.

Armstrong saw the expression on my face and said, 'Like it?'

'Does it,' I asked, 'have the mechanical ability to travel at less than eighty miles an hour?'

He laughed aloud at my question, opened the front passenger door and, with a certain amount of exaggerated dash, stood aside to allow me freedom to climb inside.

We drove at what (by Aston Martin standards) was a very moderate speed, until we arrived at a house on the outskirts of the town. A very handsome house; a fine example of Victorian architecture, without that exaggerated frippery which so often destroys much of the beauty of that period's building-style. It stood in its own acre or so of garden, and the broom and the honeysuckle and the fuchsias in the beds spaced around the well-kept lawns gave evidence of a love of horticulture. A fine house, with a fine garden. Indeed, for the widow of an ex-detective sergeant ...

Armstrong, it seemed, could also read minds.

He said, 'Bowling bought it for a song. It had been standing empty for almost three years ... perhaps more.'

'Indeed?'

'And before that – oh, for years – it belonged to three spinster sisters. They let it go to rack and ruin. Bowling bought it for a song.'

I nodded. Today it would have cost more than a song. Today it would have cost something approaching *Der Ring Des Nibelungen* ... with *Aïda* thrown in as conveyancing fee.

We'd left the Aston Martin and were walking up the path. When we reached the door, Armstrong pressed the bell-push, the door opened and for the first time I saw Kathleen Bowling.

SEVEN

Kathleen Bowling was one of the most magnificent women I'd ever . . .

No. That's incorrect. That gives a wrong impression; a wrong impression of *me*. Discounting my colleagues at the Bar (those on the distaff side) I have known few women. The wives of friends perhaps; but, as such, merely appendages to whom one must be polite. Clients, but as I've already explained, my normal habit was to meet a client for the first time in court. Witnesses . . . little more than voices from a witness box, to be coaxed or cross-examined, as the situation demanded. But women *as* women? Not since my university days had I consciously noted the physical appearance of a woman.

I noted the physical appearance of Kathleen Bowling. She was not young. I hadn't expected her to be young. She was, perhaps, in her late forties – possibly in her early fifties – and at a guess life had been more than unkind to her. It was there to see; the scars of suffering; the marks which only come when a person has fought a way through a personal hell. The mid-brown hair was streaked with grey. The 'crow's feet' around the outer corners of the eyes. And the eyes were slightly sunken in their sockets, with a touch of darkness on the surrounding skin. The mouth: thin, level and with only the hint of lipstick. And the jaw was slightly out-thrust; a determined jaw; a quietly defiant jaw.

Armstrong said, 'Kate. This is Mr Whitehouse, Q.C.'

Mrs Bowling nodded a greeting and we shook hands. She had a cool hand and a firm grip.

As we entered the house, as she led us to the lounge,

44

as Armstrong talked polite banalities, I watched this woman and, from externals, tried to form some sort of opinion. She held herself well; with pride and making the most of her average height. She was large boned, but not *heavy* boned; the frame was strong enough to carry the flesh with comparative ease, and the flesh included enough controlled muscle to ensure a good carriage. Her step was as firm – as cool and as controlled – as her handshake. Her voice was steady – a little deep, perhaps – and without any noticeable tremor; the fact that I was a barrister and a Q.C. in no way intimidated her. She wore a dress – not expensive, not cheap – the sort of dress which needs 'looking for'; high-necked, long-sleeved and with a skirt-length which, while not short, was not long enough to give the appearance of dowdiness. A very independent woman. A very direct woman. A woman who, in the event, would (I thought) make an excellent witness.

We reached the lounge, she offered coffee, we declined, then we seated ourselves in comfortable armchairs and Armstrong moved into the background and left the conversation to myself and Mrs Bowling.

She said, 'Smoke if you wish . . . I don't.'

'Thank you.' I took one of Armstrong's proffered cigarettes and lighted it from the flame of his lighter. He, too, lighted a cigarette, then moved a stand ashtray into a position convenient to us both. Then I said, 'Tomorrow I represent Mr Patsold.'

'Mr Armstrong told me.'

'You know Patsold?'

'Yes.' She nodded.

'Well?'

'He's my G.P.'

'No more than that?'

'I'm sorry. I don't understand.'

'Your local doctor. That's how well you know him? No more than that?'

'He's a friend. I know him. I know – *knew* – his wife.'
'As a friend? Patsold, I mean.'
'This is a small community, Mr Whitehouse. Everybody knows everybody.'
'Nevertheless, Patsold was – still is – your friend?'
'Yes.'
'Have you ever met him socially? *Not* as a medic?'
'Oh, yes, in the past.'
'The past?'
'Years ago. When my husband was alive, when he was in the force.'
'But not since?'
'Not socially.'
'Any particular reason?'
'Mr Whitehouse.' The quick smile was a little grim, a little sardonic. 'I'm a widow. To many people, that equates with "merry" . . . which I'm not. To many other people it means I'm fair game in the amateur match-making stakes. If anything I like that even less.'
'You have private means?' I probed gently.
'Some.' Her eyes narrowed fractionally. 'A small cheque from the building society each month. This house – and its contents – were paid for while my husband was alive. I work, full-time, at the local public library. Does that answer all the questions you were going to ask?'
'Very adequately,' I smiled.
There was a silence then I said, 'You've been – er – ill?'
'A mental breakdown. *Two* mental breakdowns. That's the popular euphemism.'
'Only a euphemism?' I raised my eyebrows in polite surprise.
'I tried suicide . . . once,' she said heavily. 'I couldn't even do *that*. You want the truth? On both occasions I should have been certified.'
'But weren't?'
'No.'

46

'Why not?'

'Jerry pulled me through.'

'Patsold?'

She nodded.

I said, 'Without – so I'm told – specialised assistance.'

'He's a damn good doctor.' She made it a simple statement of fact.

'Therefore you have cause to be grateful?'

'I am grateful. *Very* grateful.'

I drew on the cigarette, tapped ash into the ash-tray, then asked, 'What about his wife?'

'Beth?' A tiny curl touched her lips as she spoke the name.

'Patsold's wife.'

'She was a silly little cow.'

'What makes you . . .?'

'But he *didn't* kill her.'

'What makes you call her that?' I completed the question.

'A silly little cow?' She smiled. It was not a pleasant smile.

'You must have a reason.'

'She was one of the "merry widow" fraternity.'

I waited. As any professional asker of questions will testify, there are times when the answer must not be pressed. Times when it is better – easier and more productive – to wait for an addendum to the previous answer. This I did, and the addendum came.

In a low voice, which contained bitterness, she said, 'She was so bloody sure. We were bed-hopping.'

'Lovers?' I asked gently.

'That's what *she* thought.'

'And were you?'

'Oh, for God's sake!'

'She must have had a reason,' I insisted.

'Look, you don't know . . .'

'Or *thought* she had a reason.'

'You don't know Jerry.'

'You *do*?'

'Certainly. He was my . . .'

'Your G.P.' I ended the sentence for her. 'Mrs Bowling, people usually know their doctor less intimately than they know their milk-delivery man. You claim to know yours socially, but not his wife.'

'I knew her socially, too. It was necessary.'

'In order to know him?'

She frowned, hesitated, then grudgingly said, 'Yes . . . I suppose so. I hadn't thought of it that way. But I suppose so.'

Again it was time for a pause. This was not a cross-examination. If anything it was a conversation piece; a desire to understand; a gentle probing into Kathleen Bowling's mind as a first step towards understanding the mind of Gerald Patsold. I therefore gave her time to consider her last remark.

Then, as gently as possible, I said, 'Are you in love with Patsold, Mrs Bowling?'

'I've already told you . . .'

'Not have you *made* love. Are you *in* love.'

There was an infinitesimal hesitation, then she said, 'No . . . of course I'm not,' but the answer had that low, muttered quality so often associated with self-disgust. In a stronger voice she added, 'I'm past the starry-eyed age of "falling in love", Mr Whitehouse.'

Armstrong cleared his throat and interposed a question for the first time.

'Excuse me, sir.' Then to the woman, 'Would you *know*, Kate?'

'What?' She almost snapped the counter-question back at him

'If you were in love with Jerry . . . would you know?'

'That's a ridiculous question.'

'No, madam. A very erudite question.' I smiled my appreciation of Armstrong's wisdom. This young man

48

was unusually keen-witted. I continued, 'Your age . . .
it does not preclude you from falling in love. But it
might – in certain circumstances – force you into a
denial.'

'You mean I'm lying?' She was becoming angry.

'Not deliberately,' I soothed.

'In that case . . .'

'Mrs Bowling.' I tried to put it as diplomatically as
possible. 'Twice – you've just told us – you've suffered a
severe nervous breakdown. An illness. A mental illness.
You're recovered – of course you are – but your recovery has, twice, been due to Patsold's skill and care.'

She nodded.

'You must feel you owe him *something*.'

'I – I owe him *everything*,' she whispered.

'Gratitude?'

'More than that.'

'More than gratitude?'

Once more she nodded; an unhappy, almost shameful,
movement of the head.

'Love?' I suggested softly.

'Not what you mean,' she breathed.

'I mean love,' I assured her. 'I don't mean sex.'

She raised her head, looked at me and, in a heart-
broken tone, said, 'Why couldn't *she* see that?'

'Patsold's wife?'

'Why the hell,' she whispered, 'couldn't she *understand*?'

EIGHT

'A character witness?'

Armstrong made it part question, part statement.
And the questioning part did not admit of a ready

49

answer. Certainly, Kathleen Bowling would have stepped into any witness box and, quite happily, given Patsold a character reference second only to the Almighty. Indeed, Marty had suggested as much.

Armstrong drove the Aston Martin slowly – deliberately slowly – as we debated the possibility of using Kathleen Bowling as a Defence witness.

'Babies and bathwater,' I remarked with a wry smile.

'I know.' Armstrong frowned at the road ahead, then asked, 'How does Clipstone cross-examine?'

'Fairly . . . but hard.'

'She'll fold,' he sighed.

'No. She won't fold. She'll overstate her case, then they'll recall Webb and *he'll* demolish her.'

'We could object.'

'To the recall of Webb for rebuttal evidence? No.' I shook my head. 'Belmont's a good judge. He wouldn't allow the objection.'

'It might be worth the gamble.'

'No.' I was very dogmatic. Armstrong was good – for his age – but *I* had the experience. I knew courtroom play much better than he did. Almost as an afterthought I added, 'Webb would use her as a vehicle for headlines.'

I could feel Armstrong's sudden realisation. Odd, it happens sometimes. 'Vibes' is the manner of description in the modern idiom. Meaning vibrations, I suppose. I wouldn't dismiss it as one more stupidity in an age which has a surfeit of stupidities. There is, I think, enough truth in it for partial acceptance.

Sometimes in court . . . This feeling – these 'vibes' – there is no obvious reason, nothing dramatic has happened, and yet there is this instantaneous knowledge. You've won. You've lost. Nothing more need be said. No other witness need be called. 'Vibes' . . . from the jury, perhaps. From somewhere. Or somebody. It can either depress or elevate you . . . because you *know*. Nor am I alone. Colleagues have told me that they, too, have been party to this inexplicable certainty.

And the 'vibes' were coming from Armstrong.

'You really *hate* Webb . . . don't you?'

It was a statement of fact. The suffix question merely expressed surprise. Even amazement.

'I've known him a long time,' I hedged. 'We were at university together.'

'Oh, I see.'

'In his own field outstanding. One might almost say unique.'

'Quite.'

That was all. He didn't pry. He didn't probe. I think he realised he'd touched a nerve and was sensitive enough not to press the point. It made me even more appreciative of this young solicitor; this man of an age to be my own son and of whom, had he been my son, I would have been proud.

For what was left of our journey we drove in silence.

NINE

Tell me . . . can a building be arrogant? I don't mean proud; I have seen many examples of fine architecture in the capital, and their proportions, coupled with their perfection of line, immediately conjures up the word 'pride'. But that is not what I mean. I mean *arrogance*. The shape, the size, the beauty or even the ugliness, have nothing to do with it. It is the building . . . and, perhaps, the purpose to which that building is put. And to me there is arrogance. There is a hint of tyranny, more than a little contempt and something which can only be called brazenness.

The building itself tries to crush by its very presence.

Standing there – before you even enter it – it seems to try to intimidate you.

Some newspaper offices have this quality. Some court-houses. And not a few police stations. Pendlebridge Police Station had it in abundance.

The uniformed constable at the public counter knew Armstrong. He smiled a reluctant greeting as he opened the door in the wall alongside the counter to allow us access to the 'official' part of the building.

He said, 'Inspector Leroy's in his office. He's expecting you.'

There was no friendliness in the constable's tone and, as I passed, I could feel the scowl of curiosity. I was a barrister (*and* from London); I was a Q.C.; I was the lawyer (the *shyster* lawyer) who, given half a chance, would allow Patsold to get away with murder. The accusation was not voiced. No words left the constable's lips and I did not even look at his face. But like the transmission and reception of a radio message, it was sent and received.

Armstrong knew his way around the police station. I followed him along a labyrinth of corridors and up a flight of stairs. He tapped at a door then, without waiting for the invitation to reach us, opened the door, and we entered Leroy's office.

It was a typical C.I.D. inspector's office. Sparsely furnished; table-desk, swivel-chair, green-painted filing cabinet, coat-rack, two extra tubular-steel and canvas chairs, waste-paper basket. The floor was of deep red composition, polished until it presented a possible hazard to unwary walkers. There was a picture-window behind Leroy's chair which looked out on to the flat roof of some other part of the police station. The office smelled of air-freshener and wax polish.

Armstrong closed the door and performed the introductions.

For a police officer Leroy was a small man; at a guess

he must have *just* scraped through the regulation height. Nevertheless, he was stocky, with the hint of unwanted fat around the waist. At some time in the past he must have suffered a terrible injury to his upper lip; it had been torn from left nostril to centre and had been stitched without too much skill. The result was a scar (much like the scar resultant upon surgery for a cleft palate, but infinitely worse) which lifted the lip, showed a glimpse of teeth and gave the impression of a permanent sneer. I estimated his age as about midway between that of Armstrong and of myself; his close-cropped hair was of ginger-tinged brown, but liberally flecked with grey. He was, very obviously, 'off duty'; he wore army twill slacks, sandals, an open-necked short-sleeved towelling shirt and, at the V of the neck, an abundance of curly chest-hairs pushed aside the restriction of the material.

We shook hands; a firm handshake and I had the feeling that the spatulate fingers could, if necessary squeeze until the bones of my own hand snapped under the pressure. He had blue eyes; that slightly-lighter-than-forget-me-not-blue which is rare, but which is sometimes seen in men and women with ginger hair.

He waved a hand and said, 'Pull the chairs up. The superintendent wants us to co-operate.'

Armstrong and I pulled the tubular-steel chairs close to the desk, and I allowed Armstrong to start the conversation.

'This co-operation,' said Armstrong carefully. 'Does it extend to letting us see the file on Patsold?'

Leroy leaned sideways, opened a lower drawer of the desk, took out a neatly bound folder and slapped it on to the desk top.

'Co-operation, the man said.' He grinned and the sneer transformed itself into a friendly grimace. 'I knew Patsold. He was my own medic. I do my job, but I don't always like it.'

'You think he's innocent?' I asked gently.

'Mr Whitehouse, if I didn't think he was guilty he wouldn't be in a holding prison.'

'*Might* he be innocent?' I pressed.

'I don't think so.' He did not enjoy having to give a truthful answer. 'I don't see how the hell he *can* be.'

Armstrong said, 'He never admitted it, though, did he?'

'He said it must have been him.' Leroy moved his shoulder. 'If that's not an admission . . . okay, he didn't admit it.'

'Who questioned him?' I asked.

'Me. Every time.'

'A prolonged interrogation?'

'An hour. About an hour. No more.'

'That's not very long . . . for a murder enquiry.'

'An *enquiry*?' The torn lip moved, and he shook his head slowly. 'Any enquiry, and *I* wouldn't be the main officer in the case. Any doubt at all . . . this place would have been top-heavy with rank. A handful of statements. That's all it needed.'

'Did Patsold make a statement?' I asked.

'No.'

'Why not?'

'Look, sir, you want the truth?' He tapped the file with a forefinger. 'In there there's enough to send him down. There was no digging. No need for digging. It was there to pick up. I questioned him. As a working jack, but also as a friend. I could have fixed him . . . nothing surer. He was punch-drunk. I could have conned him into saying *anything*. He said just what's recorded . . . that it *must* have been him. The usual . . . he was "invited" to make a statement. He was cautioned, then asked. He asked *me* for advice. Off the record . . . I told him *not* to.'

'Why?' I asked.

'He was my friend. He was up to the eyeballs in

54

trouble already.' He stared – almost glared – at me with those blue eyes of his, then said, 'Mr Whitehouse, you know the score. Me? In his shoes I'd have had my arms torn out before I'd have given a statement.'

'You have a poor opinion of your colleagues,' I murmured.

'Some,' he agreed gruffly. 'But in this nick, we don't do things on the twist. *I* see to that.'

'We're fortunate.'

'It's not the only nick.' Suddenly he was on the defensive. I must not cast doubt upon the honesty of his fellow-officers. 'The bad bastards get all the newspaper coverage. The rest of us suffer.'

'Nevertheless . . .'

'Nevertheless, Mr Whitehouse, Jerry Patsold strangled his wife. And, unless you pull some technical blinder, I can prove his guilt right to the hilt.'

'No technical blinders, inspector,' I smiled. 'But you made a mention of his state. "Punch-drunk" was the expression you used.'

'He was that,' agreed Leroy.

'When you arrived?'

'Uhuh.' Leroy nodded. His mind was ahead of my next question and he continued, 'His son found 'em. Dialled nine-nine-nine. I was in the first car to arrive at the scene. At my guess he'd killed his wife within the last fifteen – no more than twenty – minutes. He was in a state of shock.'

'Patsold?'

'Him and his son . . . both.'

I tried to visualise the scene. In truth, I couldn't. Barristers, like surgeons, see little of the terror and wretchedness which is the curtain-raiser to their own appearance on stage. The gown is settled across the shoulders, the wig is adjusted to give comfort, but by that time the man (or woman) who is to climb into the dock is often past caring. There is, I think, an emotional threshold; a point beyond which numbness takes over and a state of unreality prevails. I had seen it so often. The lifeless eyes. The drooping shoulders. The complete non-interest in either trial or verdict. No, I tried, but I could *not* visualise Patsold (or, indeed, anybody) within minutes of committing a murder.

'The details, inspector, please,' I urged. 'I am not doubting you . . . not for a moment. But the details – however unpleasant – *are* important.'

'There are photographs.' Leroy once more tapped the closed file.

'Ah, yes, but *before* the photographs were taken. When you arrived. When you walked into the room. What did you see?'

'Well, now . . .' Leroy leaned back in his chair, linked his fingers across his stomach and stared at the ceiling as he concentrated his memory. 'The woman – Patsold's wife – was on the floor. On the hearthrug. She was dead. The rules and regulations say we have to have medical verification – and we did, from his partner, Dr Grace – but *I* know a corpse when I see one. She was dead. Blue-faced. Tongue protruding. Marks on the neck. She'd been strangled . . . that much was obvious. He'd used some strength. "Berserk" is the word that springs to mind. His nail-marks were on her throat. Deep. She hadn't been dead long . . . blood was still seeping from the gouge-marks in her neck.

'There'd obviously been one hell of a fight. A stand-lamp was over and smashed. And a table – a small but heavy coffee-table thing – and a vase of flowers which had been on the table. The vase was smashed. The water was all over the carpet. The flowers were scattered. Oh, yes, and a chair had been overturned and broken. She'd struggled, and they'd moved just about all over the room. As I say, it had been a hell of a fight.'

'And the son?' I asked.

'He was in the hall waiting for us. Sitting on a chair

56

alongside the telephone table. Trembling. Shaking like a leaf. He's a junkie and . . .'

'You *know* that?' I interrupted.

'We've nailed him once.' Leroy glanced at Armstrong. 'He got away with it. But he's back again . . . once you've seen 'em, you *know*. He was sitting there. Couldn't talk. Couldn't get the words out. Just waved his arm towards the door of the living room. The door was open. We went inside. That's what we saw.'

'And Patsold?'

'He was in an armchair. Knackered. Arms hanging down by the side. Head rolling around on his neck. You've seen a fighter – a heavyweight – after he's had a real thumping? Like that. And he'd *had* a thumping . . . of a sort. I've seen scratched faces, but nothing like that. She'd clawed him to ribbons. The front of his shirt – his tie, his lapels – saturated in the stuff. She couldn't have done a better job if she'd used fish-hooks.'

'And his first words?' I asked.

'Nothing.' Leroy frowned at the ceiling. 'It took us five minutes – all of five minutes – to get him to even *hear* us.'

'Was he unconscious then?'

'No. Not unconscious. His eyes were open. He was staring. Staring at me, but not recognising me. Not hearing a damn word we were saying.' He hesitated, then continued, 'I slapped him across the cheek. That's not in the report, but it gives you some idea. I slapped him – not hard, but hard enough. I think it helped, but not much. I thought he was maybe drunk. I smelled his breath. He wasn't drunk. Not a whiff.'

'He was in a stupor,' I suggested.

'That about sums it up,' agreed Leroy. 'I'd say it was shock.'

'At what he'd done?'

'I don't know.' Leroy lowered his gaze and looked directly at me. 'I don't know, Mr Whitehouse. I wish I did. Maybe shock at what he'd done, but that assumes he *knew*. On the other hand, maybe some sort of reaction to the fight. And, believe me, there'd *been* a fight. I know him. He's not a violent man. Not at all a violent man. A man like that, in a *fight* like that – and with his wife – there's a backlash. A mental recoil of some sort. I've seen it happen. Often. But never like that . . . that's the only difference.'

'And then?'

'Not a lot.' Leroy moved his hands. 'He came round . . . gradually. He didn't say much. Nobody said much. He saw his wife. It rocked him . . . rocked him enough to make him cry. That wasn't nice. What with the injuries to his face and all. I told him she was dead. Strangled. That's when he said it must have been him.'

'That *he* must have strangled her?'

'I can't put any other interpretation on the remark. He knew what we were talking about.'

'But not that he did strangle her?' I was clutching at straws, and both Leroy and I realised that fact.

'Not that he *did* strangle her,' sighed Leroy. 'I didn't put one word into his mouth. I don't work that way.'

'I'm sure you don't.'

'I don't have to.' Once more he was on the defensive. 'The nail parings – his *and* hers – he needn't have said a damn thing.'

'The fight?' I asked. 'Did anybody hear the fight?'

'Nobody. We've made enquiries . . . standard procedure. The house stands in its own grounds. The neighbours are too far away. No passer-by heard anything . . . or at least nobody we've been able to come up with.'

'Edward?' murmured Armstrong.

Leroy turned his head and looked questioningly.

'Could he have heard the fight?'

'He says not. He just arrived home, went into the

58

living room . . . and damn near passed out. Then he telephoned us.'

'You've checked?'

'As far as possible. There's a list of his known movements for the day in the file.'

'Could *he* have killed his mother?' I asked hesitantly.

'Steady the Buffs!' Leroy smiled and his mangled upper lip, in some strange way, added to the friendliness of the smile. '*We* say Patsold killed his wife. That doesn't mean we slammed the door on all other possibilities before we charged him. Edward Patsold was up there among the runners and riders, but he was eliminated. Even *his* nail parings . . . just to be sure.'

The telephone interrupted our conversation. From one half of the exchange it was possible to conclude that the call related to some crime less heinous than murder; something (it seemed) about stolen watches. Leroy snapped instructions and suggestions to some unknown 'sergeant' and, from the tone of his voice, it was apparent that, to him, the rank of divisional detective inspector carried both responsibility and power. It was a pointer. A hint. He was (and I was prepared to accept this) a fair-minded man. But at the same time a ruthless man. A man who hated criminals. When necessary, and where necessary, a hard man.

I was grateful for that telephonic interruption. It seemed to add a dimension to Leroy. Oddly enough, it also seemed to add weight to what he had already told us.

He replaced the receiver, apologised for the interruption, and waited for whatever else we wished to say.

'Patsold?' I murmured. 'And Mrs Patsold? What is *not* in the file?'

'Sorry?' He looked puzzled. I think he knew what I meant, but was buying time in which to make a decision.

'The man,' I amplified. 'Not the murderer. Your assessment of him.'

'To me, he's a murderer.' Leroy was still unwilling to commit himself.

'Co-operation, inspector,' I reminded him. 'I doubt if I'll be calling you as a witness. But he wasn't *always* a murderer. You knew him in those days. I didn't.'

TEN

In effect, the story was a repeat of the one told me by Marty. Patsold was (had been and, if I was successful, would again be) a country G.P. But not typical. He worked; worked at his patients, worked at keeping himself abreast of modern medicine and (something of a personal hobby-horse) worked at understanding the sicknesses which visit themselves upon the mind.

Pendlebridge wasn't big enough to warrant its own mental institution, therefore Patsold had been forced to nurse his handful of mental patients, on a one-to-one basis, by visiting them at their homes. A situation which necessitated two, sometimes three, visits per day. That on top of his normal surgery hours and the visits to patients suffering from physical ailments. And *that* on top of the never-ending task of self-education, via the latest textbooks and articles published in medical journals.

He had a wife and four children (two girls, two boys) but, over the years, this self-imposed pressure of work had meant that he'd seen them less and less.

'The children,' I asked. 'Edward we know about. What about the others?'

Leroy said, 'John – he's the eldest – he's out in Australia. Alice Springs way, somewhere. He just up

and left home two – maybe three – years back. No
known address. We're still trying to trace him.'

'And the two girls?'

'They're both younger than Edward. They were at the
funeral. Ruth and Anne. One's in T.V. . . . the admin
side. The other's a secretary. They share a flat in the
Hampstead area. The address is in the file.'

'But Edward stayed at home,' I murmured.

'On and off,' grunted Leroy. 'He gets the wanderlust
fairly regularly. Ups sticks and goes.'

'Where?'

'That,' said Leroy sourly, 'is something we'd *all* like
to know.'

Armstrong leaned across and picked the file from the
desk top. Leroy gave a tiny nod of acquiescence. As
Armstrong mulled his way through the papers and
photographs, I tried to build up a picture of a family.

On the surface, a respectable family. A *respected*
family. A man, his wife, his two daughters and his two
sons. The man, a medical practitioner, in a small market
town; a doctor, who over-worked himself in the cause
of his vocation; a doctor, but also a man, and a man
who, because of this over-work would, at times, tend
to be testy and perhaps a little difficult to live with. Bad
tempered, perhaps. Perhaps not . . . a point which
needed clarification.

An elder son who left home and travelled to the other
end of the earth. More than that. An elder son who,
having reached Australia, apparently cut himself off
from his family. No address. No correspondence. Even
the police couldn't trace him.

Two daughters who also left home. Who sought a new
life in London. Who travelled north for the funeral of
their mother . . . then returned to London. Neither (or
so it seemed) prepared to interrupt their new way of life
and remain at Pendlebridge, to give moral support to a
father awaiting trial for murder.

A younger son. Something of a scoundrel at a guess. Leaving home. Returning home. Going . . . nobody knew where. A drug addict. Known to the police as such. A keeper of bad company. Not the sort of son of whom parents might be proud.

The picture of a family.

And the wife?

'Elizabeth Patsold?' I said gently.

'She's dead.' Leroy's tone was gruff and non-committal.

'Were that not so,' I said, 'we wouldn't be here.'

'What is it you want to know?' He unbent a little.

'About her.'

'She was murdered.'

'That doesn't tell me much, inspector.'

'It should.' The deformed lip moved into a slow, wry smile. 'The victims of murder, Mr Whitehouse. Half of 'em – maybe more than half – deserve what they get. They live their lives, pushing their luck. Just once they push it too far.'

'Patsold's wife?'

'She was . . .' He rubbed the back of his neck, as he sought the right word. Then he said, 'Moderate.'

'What does that mean?'

'Moderately good looking. Moderately intelligent. Moderately sensible. Moderately foolish. Moderately a pain in the arse . . . to put it bluntly.'

'And,' added Armstrong, looking up from the file, 'moderately in the family way.'

'I beg your pardon?' I stared at the solicitor.

'Here.' Armstrong tapped the open file with the nail of his right forefinger. 'The pathologist's report. Cause of death . . . plus the fact that she was carrying a two-month-old foetus in her womb.'

He handed me the opened file and I, in turn, studied the official findings of the pathologist who had performed the post-mortem examination. It was all there.

The cause of death . . . manual strangulation. The fact
that she was (or had been) a healthy woman in her mid-
forties. Then – almost as an afterthought – the fact that
she was pregnant.

'A little late in life,' I observed.

'Moderately careless,' said Leroy drily.

Armstrong said, 'It could be important.'

'Women *do* get pregnant,' said Leroy. 'Even at that
age.'

'A doctor's wife.' In effect, I was talking to myself.
Itemising facts, relevant to this new information. 'The
contraceptive pill. There for the asking. Unless, of
course, she had religious objections.'

'Agnostics . . . both of 'em,' said Leroy.

'Now,' murmured Armstrong, 'if Jerry didn't strangle
her . . .'

'He did,' grunted Leroy.

'. . . we might have somebody – some unknown
somebody – with a *real* motive for murder.'

'You never give up . . . do you?' Leroy shook his head
in friendly mockery. 'Give you a tree . . . you'll argue it's
not wood. She was *married*, for God's sake. Patsold
wasn't *so* tired. Maybe she thought she was past the
pill-taking age.'

'Moderately wrong,' I smiled.

'Moderately.' Leroy returned the smile. 'Moderately
everything.'

ELEVEN

With hindsight – with that wealth of wisdom which
comes after a given event – I tend to think I *knew*, as we
rode in the Aston Martin from the police station, and
back to Armstrong's home for lunch. But honesty

63

demands that I ask spin-off questions. How much did I know? And, come to that, was it really knowledge . . . or was it wishful thinking?

I plied Armstrong with questions, as he steered the car through the traffic which almost blocked the narrow streets.

'A locum will have taken Patsold's place since his arrest?'

'Oh yes.'

'Do you know him?'

'Grace. Young Grace . . . Patsold's partner's son. He's only recently qualified.'

'Efficient?'

'Reasonably. So I'm told. He still lacks experience . . . obviously.'

'His father will be carrying him? At least to an extent?'

'I'd say so.'

'Popular?'

'Not *un*popular . . . from what I gather. Grace is liked. The son enjoys some of the reflected glory. That's how I read the situation.'

'Where's the surgery?'

'Back down the hill.' Armstrong took his eyes from the road long enough to glance over his shoulder. 'Down there . . . by the river. A purpose-built place. Two surgeries – consulting rooms – a waiting room, a pharmacy. The usual set-up.'

'A pharmacy?'

'For those who come in from the surrounding countryside. We only run to one chemist's shop. If they live a few miles out they're given the prescription and collect it on the spot. It saves driving in during the day.'

'A purpose-built place?'

'Uhuh.'

'So . . . not an annex to one of the doctors' houses?'

'No. About equal distance from each.'

'You made mention,' I reminded him, 'of Patsold's lackadaisical manner of handling drugs. Edward could get his hands on them . . . remember?'

'They both – both Jerry and Grace – wandered in and out of the pharmacy all the time. The dispenser. A retired nurse . . . a bit on the old side. A bit slow.' He paused, then continued, 'Y'see, Mr Whitehouse, we're a rural community. Things that should be done, sometimes *aren't* done. Cutting a few corners . . . that sort of thing. I've been in his surgery – say, something for a mild attack of 'flu – and I've seen drugs lying around on his desk. Drugs that should be under lock and key. Dangerous drugs. And he's left me alone in the surgery while he's gone to the dispensary to make me up a bottle of something. I could have helped myself to those drugs. Anybody could . . . that's what I mean.' There was a second pause before he asked, 'Does all this help?'

'It's possible,' I said carefully.

'I mean, does it help Jerry? Does it help us prove he didn't murder his . . .'

'The Tolson Case,' I interrupted gently.

'The – er . . .'

'R.*v.*Tolson. An 1889 decision. Queen's Bench Division. You say *not* murder – more than that, complete innocence . . . that's the case we have to use as a peg.'

'I'm sorry, sir. I don't see how a Queen's Bench decision – almost a hundred years old – can . . .'

'Law, my boy.' I smiled and, if it was a condescending smile, it was not meant to be. Already I had genuine respect for this somewhat over-enthusiastic young solicitor. I said, 'We're not detectives. Not a police force. We must, therefore, accept the evidence. And, having accepted the evidence, we must use the law. Argue. Argue a complete innocence based upon The Tolson Case.'

TWELVE

It was an excellent lunch. Armstrong had not exaggerated; his wife was a superb cook. It was, moreover, a 'Yorkshire' lunch . . . deliberately so, at a guess, in order to demonstrate to an effete Southerner exactly what was meant by 'north country cooking'. The sliced melon with brown sugar. The Yorkshire pudding served as a separate course; served in squares, and with rich, beef gravy. The main course: sirloin, cooked to perfection, new potatoes, baby carrots, fresh garden peas, broccoli tips. And, as a sweet, home-made apple pie with cream. A feast for a monarch and, as we sipped coffee and smoked after-meal cigarettes, I felt a comfortable tightness at the waistline.

I congratulated Mrs Armstrong and she smiled her thanks.

She was the perfect foil for Armstrong's extrovert nature. A woman who was within touching distance of genuine beauty, but – or so it seemed – completely unaware of that fact. Quietly spoken. Shy . . . or was it, perhaps, because of the presence at her table of such an exalted being as a Queen's Counsel? I hoped not. I thought not. It would have marred her gentle charm.

They were obviously very much in love with each other. It was there in every exchange. In every glance. In every smile. This young man appreciated his good fortune and she, in turn, was not unaware of the tiny courtesies, so often forgotten after marriage; the holding open of doors, the positioning of her chair at the table, the general politeness, the continuation of which seems, to me, that firm basis upon which every good marriage is built.

Gradually, some of the shyness left her. As we smoked and sipped coffee – as Armstrong and I exchanged opinions, spiced with gentle legal banter – some of the timidity melted. She smiled more often. She even laughed aloud – a delightful chuckling sound – at some forensic pun voiced by her husband.

Then, in a lull in the conversation – almost hesitantly she remarked, 'Your – your wife, Mrs Whitehouse, must be lonely sometimes, with you at court all day and working in chambers most evenings.'

'There is no Mrs Whitehouse,' I said.

'Oh!' Her face reddened.

'There never was, my dear.' I smiled away her embarrassment. 'I'm one of those old-fashioned bachelor types. I've – er – I've never had the courage to pop the question.'

'Then *you* must be lonely,' she said simply.

'Sometimes,' I admitted.

Armstrong said, 'It's never too late.' And from the tone – from the manner in which he made what was, on the surface, a jocular remark – I think he realised that inadvertently his wife had touched a curtain I would have wished to remain closed.

'Never,' I agreed with a half-smile. 'Nothing is ever too late.'

But it *was* . . .

Thirty years too late. A mild, undergraduate orgy too late. And – if the truth *had* to be faced – a life-long friendship, which had never been a *real* friendship, too late.

And at that moment, at the dining table of a Pendlebridge solicitor's house – in the company of a charming young man and his equally charming wife – having been their guest at table and eaten a magnificent lunch . . . at that moment I *knew*.

Patsold didn't matter. Patsold was a means to an end. He was innocent; Armstrong had convinced me of his innocence. But neither his guilt nor his innocence was of major importance. Only Marty was important. Marty and the fact that I was determined to grind him into nothingness. To destroy him. To discredit him. To make the eminent Dr Martin Webb, Professor of Psychology and Criminal Psychiatry, the laughing stock of all his peers. This was why I'd feigned friendship for all these years . . . *for this case.*

Such stupidity! Such crass arrogance! The friendship had *been* a friendship. A genuine friendship. A friendship of opposites, perhaps, but no less firm a friendship for that. As for the Patsold case . . . another case, no more no less. Certainly not a great case. Certainly not an *important* case. One more case . . . that was all. I had accepted a change of plea, but barristers *do* accept changes of plea. Patsold was innocent. Was he? Armstrong thought so. More than thought so. Was convinced. Well, Armstrong knew Patsold, and I in turn had come in a very short time to value the opinion of Reginald Armstrong. Via him I had received my instructions . . . Patsold was innocent.

So be it.

But the idea of carrying a secret hatred for thirty years, of prolonging a pretence of friendship for all that time . . . it was ridiculous. Outrageous. Unworthy of my own profession.

Armstrong had pushed back his chair, was on his feet and saying, 'A glass of iced water, perhaps?'

'I – er – I beg your pardon?' I shook my head slightly, in an effort to rid myself of warring thoughts.

'You look ill, sir. I thought you were going to . . .'

'Lack of sleep, my boy.' I tried to smile. 'The years take their toll.'

'I'm – I'm sorry. *Very* sorry.'

'Don't be.' I was my normal self once more. I turned

to the worried-looking Mrs Armstrong. 'You too, my dear, please. Ignore the small weaknesses of a somewhat staid man of law. We bachelors.' Again I smiled. This time a true smile in an attempt to put her at ease. 'Not just last night, you understand. Too many nights . . . far too many nights. As you were wise enough to remark. A wife would have put her foot down.'

She returned my smile, with a hint of sadness attached. Then, almost hesitantly, she reached out and closed the fingers of one hand over the back of my own. It was a beautiful, silent token of friendship. The slight squeeze before she withdrew her hand. Had I had a daughter, I might have hoped for such a gesture. Or, if not a daughter, a favourite niece. I had neither, but instead I had Ruth Armstrong.

Armstrong was still on his feet. Still looking worried.

He said, 'We could cancel this afternoon's interview with . . .'

'Not see Edward Patsold?' I injected the question with mild outrage.

'If you're not well, sir. *I* could . . .'

'My dear boy, you couldn't ask the right questions.' I moved a hand in what was (I fear) a slightly dramatic gesticulation. 'Tomorrow. In court. *I* shall be conducting the advocacy. The questions I ask – the questions I ask to witnesses other than Edward Patsold – will depend upon his replies of today. His replies and the manner of those replies.' I turned to Ruth Armstrong and continued, 'And you, my dear. Instructions from a man in whom your husband stands in some awe. While we go about our dreary business you will telephone the best restaurant in town. The very best, you understand? And you will book a table for three – we three – for dinner. And this time you will both honour me by being *my* guests.'

THIRTEEN

Edward Patsold was waiting for us at his home; a severe-looking, stone-built house standing in its laurel-heavy garden. At the front – alongside the drive – there had once been a lawn, but the grass was now almost twelve inches high and polka-dotted with meadow buttercups. Like the lawn, the house had been neglected. And yet there was about the place an air of past happiness; of a happiness which had been laughter-filled and complete but which, for some reason, had gone sour.

Edward Patsold answered our ring and led us along passages to the kitchen of the house. A huge kitchen, with a corresponding array of modern gadgetry and Formica-faced working surfaces. I know little about kitchens, but even I could appreciate that many housewives would have looked upon that kitchen as an annex to Heaven itself.

A few scattered chairs were at our disposal and, having seated ourselves, Edward Patsold lifted a half-consumed tin of beer from the tiled floor alongside his chair, and poured some of the liquid down his throat. He was an unprepossessing youth; of a generation and of a kind. His hair was shoulder-length, untrimmed and uncombed. Unless he was scruffy to a degree which precluded him from shaving, other than once a week, he was in the first throes of growing a beard. He wore a lightweight, turtle-necked sweater with long sleeves, stained jeans and open-toed sandals. The word 'hippy' sprang to mind but, from the few I'd met in the course of my professional life, I guessed that they would have

70

disowned him as one of their number; the hippies *I* had met had (indeed) sported a surfeit of hair, but to their credit it had been clean and, as far as possible, moderately well coiffeured.

He sat drinking beer and scowling at us. His narrow, pale-complexioned face seemed to be the dwelling place of an everlasting, universal hatred. And that hatred was, for the moment, directed at Armstrong and myself; the deep-sunk eyes in their darkened sockets glared defiance as he waited for the opening gambits of our conversation.

And Armstrong opened that conversation. By previously agreed tactics, the solicitor was to start the questioning ... and then, at the appropriate moment, I would take over.

Armstrong slipped the catch of his brief-case, smoothed the virgin surface of a foolscap pad, slipped a ballpoint from an inside pocket, then said, 'You were first at the scene . . . right?'

'I've said so,' muttered Patsold.

'Not to us.' Armstrong smiled a tight little smile.

'Ask Leroy.'

'We already have.'

'So why ask me?'

'We like things first-hand.'

'I don't *have* to tell you a thing.'

'That's true,' agreed Armstrong gently.

'I could tell you to blow. Both of you.'

'True again.'

'Patsold,' I said gently. 'Tomorrow – the day after, sometime within the next few days – you'll be in a witness box. Under oath. You can, as you put it, tell us to "blow". But – and this I promise – how *you* behave today will determine how *I* behave when I cross-examine you.'

'Meaning?' The first flicker of apprehension touched the back of his eyes.

'I'll skin you alive,' I promised flatly. 'I'll turn that

71

witness box into a torture chamber . . . and when I've finished Detective Inspector Leroy will be waiting for you. And this time you will *not* be acquitted on a legal technicality.'

Armstrong stood up, placed the foolscap pad on the seat of his chair and stepped towards Patsold. He grabbed the youth's left wrist, held the arm rigid and, despite wrigglings from Patsold, pushed the sleeve of the sweater high above the elbow. There was nothing.

'He was holding the can of beer in his *left* hand,' I murmured.

'What the bloody hell . . .?'

Armstrong ignored the protests, caught the youth's right wrist and once more rolled up the sleeve of the sweater. They were there. The small bruises, with the red, pin-prick-size centres. On the inside skin of the arm, above and below the bend of the elbow. Half a dozen . . . at least half a dozen.

'Now that,' said Armstrong grimly, 'is something Inspector Leroy would give his pension to see.'

'You've no bloody right . . .'

'Main-lining. Popping. What do you call it these days?'

The youth closed his mouth and his lips became a tight line beneath his quivering nostrils.

Armstrong said, 'Do you answer questions? Or do I telephone the police station and invite Leroy to join the party?'

An answer to the question was quite unnecessary. There was complete and utter capitulation in Patsold's expression. There was, of course, hatred there too. That abnormal and erratic hatred peculiar to addicts; a hatred which, while orientated towards a specific target (in this case Armstrong and myself), is also wide-ranging enough to encompass anything which might take the fancy of a drug-dulled mind.

Armstrong returned to his chair, took up the foolscap pad and rapped questions at the subdued but surly

72

Patsold. Questions to which we knew the answers. Unimportant questions. His age, his full name, his home address . . . that sort of thing. It was a deliberate ploy. It was meant to emphasise our own command of the situation and, at the same time, to frustrate Patsold to the point where some indiscretion might slip out.

Then I took over the questioning, and Armstrong settled back to record the answers.

I said, 'You've already been asked. This time, answer. *You* were first at the scene?'

He nodded.

'Were you?' I pressed for an answer.

'Yes. I found 'em.'

'What time?'

'When I got home.'

'The *time*?' I insisted.

'About eightish . . . maybe a bit after.'

'Half past eight?'

'No. Before then.'

'Fifteen minutes past eight?'

'About that. Between eight and quarter past.'

'You came in at the front door?'

'Yes.'

'Straight through the hall and into the living room?'

'Yes.'

'No stops on the way?'

'No . . . no stops.'

'You opened the living-room door. Then what?'

'I saw 'em. Then telephoned for the coppers.'

'Just like that?' I gave the question a sneering quality.

'Eh?'

'Cool, calm and collected?'

'What do *you* think?' This time *his* question was a sneer.

'You opened the living-room door. You saw the scene. Then what? No generalisations. Step by step Second by second. What did you see? What did you do?'

73

'She was – she was on the floor.'

'Your mother?'

'On the floor. On the rug. With everything smashed.'

'There'd been a fight?'

'On the floor. On the rug.' His sunken eyes stared into the far distance and I knew he was seeing, once again, the carnage he'd been faced with when he opened the living room door. He whispered, 'She was – she was *awful.*'

'Blue-faced?'

I used a dry, monotonous tone. Without feeling. Without compassion. My task was to break the spirit of this foolish young man; to break the dam of his emotions and, by so doing, perhaps force him to tell us some tiny detail the police had missed.

'Blue-faced?' I repeated.

He nodded.

'Bloated-faced?'

Once more he nodded.

'Eyes protruding?'

For a third time, he nodded, and I could see the muscles around the corners of his mouth twitch.

'Tongue protruding?'

'Yes.' It was a whispered groan.

'Did you recognise her as your mother?'

'Yes, I . . . No! Not at first.' His face seemed to fold in upon itself. Then the tears came. Great tears, which spilled from his eyes and rolled down his cheeks unheeded. In a choking voice he repeated, 'The bastard! The bastard! The bastard!'

And now he was mine. I could work him like a potter working well-kneaded clay. I could turn him into a vessel which held not merely the truth, but the *whole* truth.

'She was dead?' I still used the toneless voice.

'The bastard killed her.'

'Why?'

'I dunno. I don't *know*.' The sniffling – the wretched-
ness – had no effect upon me.
'Did they often fight?'
'No. For Christ's sake . . .'
'Argue?'
'Eh?'
'Did they often *argue*?'
'I've – I've just said . . .'
'To argue isn't to fight. Did they often *argue*?'
'No. Very rarely.'
'But sometimes?'
'Yes . . . sometimes.'
'Rarely? Or very rarely?'
'I dunno. Sometimes. Just . . . *sometimes*.'
'Your father. Is he a violent man?'
'Look – for Christ's sake . . .'
'Is he a violent man?' I snapped a repeat of the
question.
'No. This was the first time I'd ever seen him . . .'
He stopped in mid-sentence.
'What?'
'Y'know.'
'No . . . tell me.'
'She was a pain.'
'Your mother?'
'He shoulda slapped her down. Christ . . . she wanted
everything.'
'Everything?'
'Look . . .' He stared at me, his face streaked with
tears, a dribble from his nose hanging from his upper
lip. A disgusting sight in his blubbering wretchedness
but – and of this I had no doubt – about to tell what he
believed to be the truth. He stammered, 'The – the
stupid bastard. Work . . . see? That's all. The old lady
. . . she couldn't see that. She wanted out. Dedicated
quack . . . all that crap. She wanted out. See? Some life?
Some fun outa life. She wanted . . . out.'

'Out?' I teased. 'By that expression you mean what?'
'Some fun,' he repeated. 'On the town, once in a while. Maybe a cruise. She kept on at him about a cruise. Some *fun*.'
'And your father refused?'
'Yeah.' He drew the back of his hand across his upper lip, then said, 'Well . . . *no*. Not exactly.'
'Be exact,' I said.
'He wouldn't go . . . see? That's all. The old lady could go. A cruise . . . anything. Maybe take Anne or Ruth. Maybe both. But *he* wouldn't go.'
'And that caused friction?'
'Friction?'
'Arguments?'
'Boy . . . sometimes!' He shook his head in disgust. 'The old lady. She went bonzo sometimes. The old you-don't-love-me crap. The whole works. Y'know . . . they slept in separate bedrooms. That for almost a year. The old lady. She went bananas . . . didn't give a hell who heard.'
'And your father?'
'He took it . . . most of it. Sometimes – maybe when he'd had a rough day – he'd snap back a little. But not much. He'd walk out of the room. Yeah . . . he'd walk away from it, instead of slapping her down. The stupid bastard. He couldn't see.'
'See what?'
'She was giving him a name . . . right? Making him look a real yo-yo. He shouldn't have taken it all. He shoulda smacked her in the mouth. I would . . . that's for sure.'
'He killed her,' I said flatly. Grimly.
I made it sound like an already-established statement of fact. I wanted an immediate reaction.
In a heavy voice he said, 'Yes . . . I guess a fuse blew.'
'As simple as that?'
'What else?'

76

'Using your own personal yardstick,' I agreed, 'a fuse blew.'

'What else?' he repeated . . . and there was genuine sadness in his voice for the first time.

I said, 'To go back to the moment when you opened the living-room door. Your father. Where was he?'

'In the chair.'

'The armchair?'

'The poor old sod.' Again his eyes went out of focus. Again the tears began to roll down his cheeks.

'In the armchair?' I repeated.

He nodded.

'What was he doing?'

'Just, y'know, sitting there.'

'Doing what?'

'Nothing. Just sitting there.'

'Looking at your mother?'

'No. Just sitting there. Bent forward, with his elbows on his knees.'

'Staring. Is that what you mean?'

'I dunno. He had his face in his hands.'

'Covering his face?'

'Yeah.' He nodded, slowly and sadly.

'What about the scratch marks?' I asked.

'Where?'

'On his face. Where your mother had clawed him.'

'I – I wouldn't know. I didn't see no claw-marks.'

'*Would* you have seen them?' It was a point which had to be pressed.

'Maybe.' He sniffed, then said, 'No . . . maybe not. He had his whole face covered.'

'Crying?' I asked. 'Sobbing?'

'I dunno. I don't think so. Just dumb. Numb. Y'know . . . like he didn't know hell from breakfast-time. Nothing!'

'Did he speak to you?'

'No. He didn't even know. He didn't even *see* me.'

77

'Did *you* speak to *him*?'

'Eh?'

I said, 'You're there at the doorway. Your mother's dead on the floor. Your father's in a chair with his face in his hands. There's obviously been a fight . . . a violent fight. You must have said something.'

'No.' Patsold shook his head.

'*Something*,' I insisted.

'I . . .' He ran his fingers through his unkempt hair. 'Maybe. Maybe I screamed . . . or something. Maybe that. I don't remember.'

'Your father didn't turn his head?'

'He didn't hear. Nothing. Supposing I screamed – I dunno, but supposing I *did* – nothing! I tell you. He was *dead*.'

FOURTEEN

By this time I knew I'd dragged more from Edward Patsold than had the police. In the first place, the police were his enemies whereas I, although not a friend, was, at least, astride the fence. More than that, even. In the course of his replies he had intimated that, while holding his father in some contempt, he had, nevertheless, had a certain amount of sympathy for a man with a shrewish wife. Had he been capable of love he would, I think, have loved his father more than his mother. And *I* was his father's advocate.

I had, therefore, a more perfect – a more rounded – picture than had Leroy. Of this I was certain. Equally, I was certain that Patsold could fill in some of the pre-crime blanks which, from my point of view, remained.

I allowed him a few minutes to compose himself. I offered cigarettes to both Armstrong and the youth.

They accepted them, I took one myself, then held out my lighter. I let the silence quieten the emotional atmosphere, while we inhaled and exhaled cigarette smoke, then I continued with the interrogation.

In a voice into which I injected a certain coaxing quality, I said, 'Your parents. How would you describe their relationship?'

'Separate bedrooms.' Patsold waved the hand holding the cigarette. 'Like I said.'

'That,' I smiled, 'does not, *ipso facto*, denote a breakdown in a marriage. At a certain age – in certain circumstances – it might seem a good idea.'

Armstrong raised his eyes from the foolscap pad and added, 'Your father's a doctor. That means night calls. He probably didn't want to disturb your mother.'

'Horse shit,' said Patsold bluntly.

'You sound sure,' I observed.

'You didn't know 'em.' There was disgust there. Disgust . . . and from this youth who was himself a disgusting creature.

'Tell me,' I invited.

'She was screwing around,' he said simply.

'Your mother?'

'Yeah . . . at *her* age.'

I almost smiled at this blanket condemnation of a whole generation.

I said, 'Is that an opinion? Or something you know for a fact?'

'I can count beans.' His lip curled.

'Quite. But can you name names?'

'She was getting it from somewhere. Sure as hell she wasn't getting it from the old man.'

'You being something of an expert on the subject?' This time *my* voice held contempt.

'Hey, man.' The indignation was almost laughable. 'I'm no grass green boy scout. I know what I'm . . .'

'I think you're guessing,' I mocked. 'I think you

couldn't produce one ounce of proof. Couldn't name a single name.'

'That's what *you* think.' My mockery was having the desired effect.

'I'm a lawyer,' I said coldly. 'I'm not a gossip columnist. I deal in facts, not tittle-tattle.'

'Okay.' He drew on the cigarette, blew the smoke towards the ceiling, then said, 'Take a name. Take Webb.'

FIFTEEN

My immediate reaction could be likened to that of dizziness. I heard the quick intake of breath from Armstrong, but that was of no importance. My own feeling was not of surprise. It was one of great delight in confirmation. Not (you must understand) proof. Proof of Marty's guilt needed far more than the unsubstantiated word of a dope-taking lout. Marty was a giant. Edward Patsold was less than a pygmy by comparison. I needed corroboration, and the only way I could get that corroboration was by pouring scorn upon Patsold's accusation, in the hope that he might add to that accusation.

Therefore, controlling my expression and controlling my tone, I said, 'Young man, you would be wise – and well-advised – to refrain from making such wild statements in public.'

'You don't believe?' Patsold's part-indignation and part-scorn was what I was aiming for.

'Who would?'

'For Christ's sake! Why not?'

'Professor Webb would not put his career at risk.'

' "Professor Webb wouldn't put his career at risk," '
he mocked. 'Take it from me, lawyer, Professor Webb
has the morals of a barnyard rooster.'

'And you, of course, know him so well.' I matched
mockery for mockery.

'I know him . . . and *of* him.'

'Unfortunately, I *do* know him.'

'Unfortunately?'

'For you.'

'You're his friend, eh? Buddies?'

'I know him,' I repeated.

'Yeah? Well, I know people who know him. *Really*
know him. Students from the university. They know
what he's *really* like.'

'Stupid little upstarts. Like you.'

'No. Chicks. Chicks he's tried to make. Lots of them.
Maybe he's *made* some . . . I didn't ask.'

'On the other hand, *they* could be lying.'

'Why should they lie?'

'It's been known. Notches on a gun . . . that sort of
thing. You should know why. You're of the modern
generation.'

'Okay. Okay.' He nodded his head, as if he'd reached
a decision. 'Let's say I *saw* them.'

'Webb and one of the students?'

'Webb and my old lady.'

'Your mother?'

'That's who.'

'And Webb?'

'Am I interesting you *now*?'

'If I could believe you,' I said grimly.

'*For Christ's sake!*' It was an explosion of outraged
indignation. It was what I had been waiting for; what I
had been working for; what I had been praying for. He
leaned forward in his chair, waved his arms and almost
shouted the words. 'You want an audience? You're
crazy. No way are you going to get somebody who's

81

seen. But – let me tell you, man – three, maybe four, months back. I came home unexpectedly. See? And this I *did* see. The old lady and Webb coming downstairs. From the bedroom . . . where else? And he was carrying his jacket over one arm and zipping and belting his pants. And she was in her dressing-gown and – from where I stood – damn-all else. Now, that I can tell you, mister. That I can go into any crummy witness box and swear to. You want more? Go somewhere else. But that much I *do* know.'

SIXTEEN

Since that Sunday afternoon at Pendlebridge I have looked back and pondered. I still ponder. Why was I so certain? What was there about the case – this particular case – which, almost from the start, had hinted (and more than hinted) that it was *the* case? So many times I have dismissed intuition; intuition is (I have argued) something claimed by women, when some wild and improbable guess has touched the truth. But if not intuition, what else?

Wishful thinking then?

Yes, a certain amount of wishful thinking must be admitted. My three decades of love/hate relationship with Marty must have produced *something*. Some invisible antennae, perhaps; some antennae emanating from the subconscious. Something waiting, watching, listening, fine-tuned to capture that first tiny echo of hoped-for guilt. Then having caught that echo (those unintentional hints) flashing the information to the brain – to the most immaculate computer of them all – and the answer being duly delivered as a certainty.

Perhaps, after all, that is what 'intuition' means.

The number of times I have back-tracked to that evening meal when Marty and I met prior to the case. The number of times! And I have a feeling – nothing concrete or strong enough to deserve the name 'knowledge', but nevertheless a very strong feeling. That after-dinner conversation. Marty's desire (perhaps a compulsive desire) to discuss the case. The 'talking to himself' manner of his speech. His determination to explain the triangle of Gerald Patsold, Elizabeth Patsold and Kathleen Bowling. His open admission that he had visited Elizabeth Patsold . . . 'to explain things to her'. And that remark of his – that typical 'Martyism' – 'And the old libido. How's that functioning these days?' And finally – or, perhaps, *not* finally – mention of that long-past episode involving Alice Pearson. Of all the memories . . . *that* memory.

Tiny straws in the wind. Dust motes caught up in a hurricane of guilt. But the antennae had identified them, and had translated them into what had grown to be a certainty.

I knew (as every barrister knows) that a guilty conscience is a force to be reckoned with. In the past it has sent more men to the hanging-shed than all the detective work in the world. It drove Crippen to flee, despite the fact that the police suspected nothing. It gave Seddon an arrogance in the witness box which, in effect, negated all the pleading of his counsel. And 'more recently' it has refused the 'moors murderer' Ian Brady the freedom of willpower even to *apply* for parole . . . whether or not he might be granted it. There are, indeed, dozens (hundreds!) of cases in which the guilty conscience has been partly responsible and, sometimes, wholly responsible for a murderer virtually bringing about his (and sometimes her) own downfall.

Thus, then, the reasons (if reasons they are) for my certainty of Martin Webb's complicity in the murder

83

of Elizabeth Patsold and, as Edward Patsold told of his mother's infidelity with Webb, I tried to ease this new piece of the jigsaw into its proper place.

Meanwhile Armstrong took over the questioning. He asked the right questions. The 'back-up' questions needed to substantiate Patsold's assertion.

The dressing-gown? Elizabeth Patsold's 'usual' dressing-gown; red candlewick; belted, no buttons.

Webb's clothing? Light-grey suit; cream-coloured shirt; grey tie.

Had Edward Patsold been seen? No; he'd entered via the rear door and walked to the hall via the kitchen; as he'd opened the door he'd seen his mother and Webb; they hadn't seen him; he'd returned to the kitchen, immediately left the house, then returned about half an hour later; he'd found his mother, fully dressed, preparing supper in the kitchen.

Had he even hinted to his mother what he had seen? No; if she wished to be a 'cross-screwing cow' that was *her* worry.

Could he be more specific about the date? No; yes; St Patrick's Day; that would be March Seventeenth; a Sunday; St Patrick's Day, because he'd been with 'a couple of Micks' and they'd been more 'Irish' than usual.

And the time of day? Early evening; maybe 'sevenish'; maybe a little later.

I glanced at Armstrong and, once more, asked the questions.

I said, 'You didn't tell your father what you'd seen?'

'No. Why should I? He wouldn't have cared anyway.'

'What makes you say that?'

'Their marriage thing.' He shrugged. 'It was all washed up.'

'I take it you knew Professor Webb?'

'Sure. The old man had brought him home a couple of times.'

I lighted a cigarette. This time I didn't hand them round. I smoked in silence for a moment; concentrating upon the wording of my next questions.

Then I said, 'Patsold, let us work from an assumption. Let us assume that the evidence against your father doesn't exist. That he *wasn't* in the living room when you opened the door. If you wish – if it will make for an easier answer to my question – let us further assume that your father knew about the affair your mother was having with Professor Webb. Accepting those assumptions would he be *your* Number One Suspect, insofar as the murder of your mother is concerned?'

'No way, man. No *way*.' The passion of his reply quavered his voice slightly. But for the first time the tone carried genuine adulthood. He said, 'Look, mister lawyer, get it straight. That guy is my old man. I *know* him. A doctor, see? All that crap about the sanctity of life. He *believes* it. His job was to *save* lives, okay? Jesus Christ, he almost killed himself doing just that.' He paused, then continued, 'Look – me? I'm a nothing. Think I don't know that? Think I'm so stupid I don't even know *that*? But the old man? Mister, I'm just about everything he *isn't*. I call him a mug. Most of my life, I've called him a mug. A crazy man for zapping himself like he does. Nothing too much. Taking all that crow shit from the old lady. Working his balls off . . . and for finks who wouldn't think twice about farting in his face. Everything. And just being glad he can *do* it. Man – I tell you – if I hadn't seen it. If I hadn't *seen* him there. No way, he just couldn't have killed.'

SEVENTEEN

Ruth Armstrong handed us sherry; good sherry which had been poured and was awaiting our return. She had (she told us) booked a table for dinner; first sitting at seven-thirty.

I thanked her and, as I lowered myself into a chair, she said, 'I've – there's a new razor, Mr Whitehouse. In the guest bathroom. And a can of shaving cream. And warm towels and a shower . . . if you think you might need . . .'

'I shall, my dear,' I interrupted gratefully. 'And I thank you for your thoughtfulness.'

In another easy chair, Armstrong slouched and scowled at his sherry.

'I know,' I smiled. I tasted the sherry, then continued, 'A mixed bag. Everybody says he couldn't. That it isn't in him. But we've done what the police couldn't do. We've unearthed the perfect motive.'

'More harm than good,' he growled.

'Oh, no.' I shook my head. 'The truth – as much of the truth as possible – it never does harm.'

Armstrong tipped almost half the glass of sherry down his throat in one quick gulp, then said, 'You think Webb?'

'I *know* Webb. The motive applies to him just as much as it applies to Patsold. The task is to *prove* Webb.'

'And at the same time, *dis*prove Jerry Patsold.'

'Prove Webb,' I said, 'and you automatically *dis*prove Patsold.'

' "The impossible takes a little longer",' he quoted

ironically. Then he frowned at me and asked, 'How well do you know Webb, sir?'

'Well. Very well.'

'You weren't surprised.'

'I wasn't at all surprised,' I agreed.

'Why not?' It was a blunt question, asked by a conscientious man faced with a wall of apparently insurmountable proof.

'At university,' I said slowly. ' "Do what thou wilt" – another quotation – Marty's rule of life.'

'Marty?'

'Martin Webb. Nobody could hold him. Nobody could tame him. With him the rules were made to be broken. He broke them all, but with panache. He wasn't a rebel. Not in the accepted sense. No wild, over-simplified political persuasions. He was only interested in life . . . . and the living thereof. Everything else was of secondary importance. He hasn't changed.'

'But – dammit – Beth Patsold. His friend's wife.'

'It would mean nothing.' I sipped the sherry. 'To Marty it would be a mere peccadillo. My young friend . . .' I sighed heavily. 'If Marty were here, in this room, sharing this excellent sherry, you couldn't convince him that going to bed with Patsold's wife was wrong. That it was even immoral. Even dishonourable. His argument – his convinced argument – would be that *she* had acted dishonourably . . . by becoming pregnant. That she deserved to die . . . because she didn't follow the rules – *his* rules – of living.'

'You mean he's crazy?' Armstrong swallowed more sherry.

'No . . . not crazy.'

'But – but wicked.' Ruth Armstrong had been listening to our exchange, and she expressed a tentative opinion. 'From what you both say . . . wicked.'

'Conventionally, my dear,' I agreed. 'But not according to Webb's mode of life.'

Armstrong almost snarled, 'He's – he's – he's . . .'

'He's Martin Webb,' I interrupted gently. 'He's a rebel . . . always has been. He's a lecher . . . always has been. And he's a psychiatrist.'

'And now a murderer.'

'Is it – is it possible?' Ruth Armstrong was trying to help. 'Hypnotism, I mean?'

'Possible,' I agreed. 'The reports record cases. But not this time.'

Armstrong said, 'Why not? If he's what you say he is . . .'

'That's *why* not.' I moved my glass gently. 'I know Marty. I've studied him . . . why I've studied him is of no importance. But hypnotism is too crude – too hit-and-miss – for his type of mind. Y'see, my children . . .' I was feeling slightly expansive. The sherry was doing its work. 'Hypnotism. The subject has to be very special. Very responsive. We're not discussing vaudeville hypnotism. Glorified parlour trickery. We're discussing *clinical* hypnotism. A controlled demonstration, showing how the mind can be manipulated. But the build-up, between the hypnotist and his subject, spans years. It has to reach a stage where merely by counting up to, say, five the hypnotist can induce the required trance. And moreover the trance is terrifyingly deep. Deep enough to make the subject see things which are not present. Deep enough for him or her to do anything – *anything* – demanded by the hypnotist.

'Now that, my young friends, may – at some future date – present the law with a neat little problem. In the wrong hands such power is deadly. But not this time. My reasons for being so sure? Well . . . let's say I know Marty. That relationship – the relationship between the hypnotist and the subject – only comes with years of patience. Patience, discipline and complete involvement . . . on both sides. That, and absolute trust. Marty couldn't do it. He could, perhaps, hypnotise . . . yes.

But only on a superficial level. There's a barrier that has to be passed. A subconscious barrier. And thank God for *that*. This side of that barrier a man – or a woman – can be made to make a fool of himself or herself. But no more than that. Beyond that barrier . . . that's where Mr Hyde lives. Oh, yes, he *can* be released. But not by dabblers. And not by men like Webb. Men to whom hypnotism is a mere superficial by-product of their calling.

'In addition there's something which – for want of a better description – we might call a natural "fail safe" mechanism. Accepting the proposition that Mr Hyde – *or* Mrs Hyde – lives behind that barrier in all of us . . . that's not enough. The breaking down of that barrier requires more than the right hypnotist. It also requires the right subject. A person who can be placed in a trance without difficulty . . . and by *that* hypnotist. These people – these readily hypnotised people – are rare. Very rare. In the main they are intelligent. Therefore, assuming they *do* meet the right hypnotist, only when they are certain of that hypnotist's trustworthiness will their mind allow exploration beyond a certain point.'

I finished my sherry, smiled, then concluded, 'A fascinating subject. In its infancy. Medically accepted, but as yet not fully understood.'

'Understood by you.' Mrs Armstrong returned my smile.

'Only as a layman, my dear. Only as a weekend gardener knows how to grow cabbages.'

'The Tolson Case,' muttered Armstrong to himself.

'Ah, yes, the Tolson Case.' I stood up from my chair. 'It has a bearing, some slight bearing, it *must* have.' I placed my empty glass on a nearby table and said, 'And now, dear lady. If you'll excuse me, I'll take advantage of that razor. And the shower and warm towels.'

EIGHTEEN

It really was an excellent restaurant. The tables were well-spaced; the conversation at one table did not impose itself upon the conversation at the next. The food could not be faulted and it was attractively presented. The service was pleasant without being obsequious. It was, indeed, a most enjoyable meal . . . or, to be strictly accurate, it should have been.

Poor Mrs Armstrong. She had a duo of poor companions. Both Armstrong and I strove to be moderately attentive company. To an extent we both failed. Armstrong (I knew) was worrying the puzzle to which I, too, was trying to find an answer. How could A force B to strangle C . . . without C being aware that he was a murderer? That was the crux of the problem. In fact, that *was* the problem. A jury's verdict depended upon us finding the answer . . . and before tomorrow.

Or were we creating a problem which wasn't even there? Were we deluding ourselves as far as Webb's guilt (and Patsold's innocence) were concerned? Halfway through the dessert – *Poire Cardinal* – I could contain myself no longer.

I said, 'Patsold's partner – Grace – do you know him?'

Armstrong nodded. His mouth was filled with ice cream and raspberry sauce.

'Well?'

He swallowed, then said, 'Yes. Very well.'

'The police. Did they search the surgery?'

'I – er – I suppose so.' He scowled concentration for a moment, then said, 'No. Dammit, they *didn't*. Or if they did it's not recorded on the file Leroy showed us.'

'A cut-and-dried case,' I murmured. 'Find enough evidence to convince a jury, then stop searching.' I looked at Armstrong and said, 'I'd like to see Patsold's surgery.'

'Tonight?' It was a question. It held no hint of surprise.

'If possible.'

'I'll fix it.' He pushed his chair away from the table. As he stood up I said, 'If it's convenient I'd like Dr Grace present. Oh and – er – my hotel. Could you telephone them, please? My junior, Smith-Hopkinson, should be arriving about now . . . he may well have arrived already. Ask the hotel to give him my compliments, and he need not postpone his bedtime on my behalf.'

'I'll do that, sir.'

He left us, and I turned to his wife and remarked, 'An energetic young man.'

'Reliable,' she said quietly. 'And . . .' She smiled. 'He's never stopped working on the case since you accepted the brief.'

'I hope he isn't disappointed.'

'I have a feeling. He won't be.'

'My dear young lady.' I gave a slightly exaggerated sigh. 'So many idols have feet of clay. I've lost cases. Many cases.'

'But not as many as you've won.'

'Mrs Armstrong . . . before your husband returns.' I was suddenly very serious. 'You know Patsold? You knew his wife?'

She nodded.

'Are we wrong?' I asked. '*Might* he have killed her?'

'Reginald doesn't think . . .'

'*Your* opinion, please,' I interrupted. 'I know what your husband thinks. I want *your* opinion.'

'She was very bitchy.' She spoke quietly but without hesitation. Her eyes went slightly out of focus, as if she was using her memory as a screen upon which images were being thrown. She continued, 'Make allowances for Jerry's work . . . and he was even more dedicated than *my* husband. She was still bitchy. She wasn't proud of him. She should have been, but she wasn't. Self-centred. I think that describes her. Self-centred to the point of being selfish. Once or twice I've heard her make cutting remarks – snide remarks – about how much Jerry thought of his patients.'

'Mrs Bowling?'

'That . . .' She shook her head as if unable to understand. 'That was a running sore. She didn't even try to understand. We're a small-town community, Mr Whitehouse. A close-knit community. Especially the so-called "professional" men. The wives, too. There aren't many secrets. We all knew about Kate Bowling. Her husband was a detective sergeant. He killed their only child. He . . .'

'Yes. I know,' I interrupted. 'I've heard the story. But what about Mrs Bowling and Patsold?'

'There was nothing in it.' Her voice was firm and confident. 'Kate Bowling isn't a silly little sexy piece. She isn't that sort. Never was. But she was a broken woman and Jerry mended her, that's all.'

'But Mrs Patsold?'

'Some people have dirty minds,' she said simply.

'I see. And Patsold himself?'

'Look . . . he was a doctor. You think *Reginald* is dedicated. By comparison he's just a normal, run-of-the-mill solicitor. Jerry really *was* dedicated. He could be brusque. Almost brutal. And why not? We have our quota of skivers . . . and he hadn't much time for bed-side politeness. But if you were ill. *That's* when you realised his value. He'd get you better. He wouldn't fob you off on to some specialist. He'd find out what was wrong. Then he'd cure you . . . if it meant going without sleep for weeks. I know. From personal experience.' She paused, looked sad for a moment, hesitated, then continued, 'We wanted a child. We thought – y'know – the details aren't important . . . but complications set in. There was a miscarriage.' Again there was a pause. A sad and wistful pause. She continued, 'Mr Whitehouse, you can't know what that *means*. In a way it brought us closer together, Reginald and me. But for months I was part of a very personal nightmare. I was incomplete. I was a failure as a wife. Nobody – nobody has a better husband, a more considerate husband – but he couldn't do anything. Jerry did. Slowly. With more patience than I thought possible.' There was another pause then, in a solemn, beautifully modulated voice, she added, 'To us, Jerry Patsold is almost a god.'

'And his wife?'

'He deserved better. Much better.' Then in an almost angry voice, 'She wasn't even *proud*.'

Armstrong rejoined us a few minutes later.

As he sat down he said, 'Fixed. Dr Grace will meet us at the surgery at about nine. Smith-Hopkinson's already booked in at the hotel. I spoke to him personally. He's quite intrigued. Asked if there was anything he could do to help.' He grinned. 'I told him you'd let him know.'

'It's possible,' I murmured.

Armstrong turned to his wife and said, 'A taxi home for you, my pet. I'm sorry . . . it's all in a good cause.'

'Another all-night session?' she asked impishly. She held her head to one side and continued, 'Tell me. Is there such a state as "law-widow"?'

'We could,' I suggested, 'take Mrs Armstrong home, then . . .'

'And do without my Camembert and coffee?' He raised theatrically shocked eyebrows. Then, as he beckoned for the waiter to bring the cheese tray, he added,

'It's all fixed, sir. I've arranged for the taxi. It should arrive here in about thirty minutes.'

'You will notice, Mr Whitehouse,' said his wife, 'that my husband is a great "fixer". One day he'll "fix" himself into a knot even *he* can't untie.'

It was, I decided, a very modern marriage. Good, and with all the right ingredients, but to an elderly codger like myself . . . a little hectic at times.

NINETEEN

For a doctor with such a reputation it was a very ordinary surgery. I had expected to find gadgetry galore – a modern counterpart to the medieval torture chamber – but not a bit of it. It was the usual run-of-the-mill medic's consulting room. The roll-topped desk, the swivel-chair, the second (less comfortable) chair for the patient, the leather-covered couch along one wall, the corner wash-basin, the glass-fronted wall-cabinet with its small array of instruments . . . the usual, slightly intimidatory paraphernalia beloved of (and one presumes necessary to) the average General Practitioner.

I apologised to Grace for any inconvenience caused, but he waved my apology aside with the stem of his pipe. It was an ancient and cracked cherrywood and, by the nauseous smell coming from its bowl, I guessed that he favoured some form of herbal tobacco.

He said, 'He's up tomorrow . . . that right?'

'Tomorrow morning,' I agreed.

'You've cut it fine.'

'We've all night,' said Armstrong and I almost shuddered. He made it sound as if sleep was a luxury; an indulgence enjoyed only by the bored and idle rich.

'Patsold's surgery?' I turned my head as I made the remark.

'Exactly as he left it.'

'Really? I understood your son . . .'

'He's using the spare consulting room.' Grace struck a match and applied the flame to the surface of whatever concoction the bowl of the cherrywood held. Clouds of evil-smelling smoke squirted from his mouth as he continued, 'We could do with a third pair of hands When Patsold's back in harness, I'll have a word. Might let the lad come in as junior partner.'

'*If* Patsold comes back into harness,' I corrected him.

'Is there some doubt?' He waved out the match and his tone and expression both carried shocked surprise.

'The police think so,' I observed.

'Them!' He snorted. 'They're bloody mad.'

'Not quite mad, doctor. Detective Inspector Leroy . . .'

'Leroy's a certifiable lunatic.'

'Indeed?'

'He can't even keep the vandals in check.'

'I'm sorry. I don't see the rele . . .'

'Daubing their lavatory-wall garbage all over my garage door.'

'Oh!'

'How in hell's name can a man incapable of handling a thing like that detect a *murder*?'

Armstrong asked, 'Did the police visit the surgery?'

'Leroy?' Grace (very obviously) nursed an obsessional dislike of Detective Inspector Leroy.

'Anybody,' said Armstrong. 'The police.'

'They haven't the simple gumption,' growled Grace. 'Park on a double yellow line and they're around you in swarms. But give 'em something a little more involved than simple addition, and they're . . .'

'So this . . .' I looked around me. 'This is how Patsold left it. *Exactly* as he left it.'

'Patsold and Webb.'

'And Webb?' I said softly.

'Patsold's friend. One of the leading nut-experts. He . . .'

'I know Webb,' I interrupted. 'He'll be giving evidence for the Prosecution.'

'Doctor . . .' Armstrong spoke more slowly than usual; enunciating each word very distinctly. 'Doctor, we would like you to cast your mind back to the evening of Tuesday, May the seventh. That was the day Patsold was arrested. The day he supposedly killed his wife. Will you please describe what happened before he left here.'

'Gladly.' Grace struck another match and the evil-smelling mixture gave off more fumes. 'Tuesday. A normal Tuesday, as I recall. Coughs and sneezes – the usual miserable parade. Oh, yes, there was a raving lunatic who'd caught his foot in the blades of his Flymo. Damn fool! It's there on the machine. All the warnings in the world. This blasted idiot either couldn't read or thought he had steel feet. Fortunately, he was wearing heavy boots. A lovely bruise, though. A beauty.' He chuckled. 'He won't belch in church again in a hurry.'

'What *happened*, doctor?' pleaded Armstrong.

'I've just said. The damn fool caught his foot in the blades . . .'

'Patsold . . . *please.*'

'Oh, yes.' Grace waved his pipe vaguely. 'Tuesday. That's double surgery. We're both here in the evening. Jerry was here . . . here in his own consulting room. I was in mine. This Flymo idiot. I remember . . . I went to the dispensary for some ointment. Webb was just coming in. The usual thing. "Hello" . . . that sort of thing. Then he wandered into Jerry's consulting room. I know. I was still in the dispensary – mixing some jollup for the Flymo lunatic – when Jerry came in to

96

check our stock of Dimotapp. Some woman – his last patient – with a runny nose.

'That was the last time I saw him. Surgery had just about finished. I know the Flymo lad was my last patient. I plastered his foot with goo, then packed up and went home. There was a light on in Jerry's consulting room when I left. But that wasn't unusual. Webb came in for a natter – usually at about the end of surgery – and they often stayed on talking. Jerry was a little wild about nut-cracking.'

'Nut-cracking?' I murmured.

'Psychology,' explained Armstrong. 'Psychiatry.'

'An odd subject.' Grace waved his pipe around as an emphasis to his opinion. 'A bit beyond me. Do either of you smoke a pipe, by the way?'

'Er . . . no.'

'Not me,' said Armstrong.

'Pity.' Grace's tone held an almost childish disappointment. 'This stuff. You'd *really* enjoy it. Home grown, home cured.'

'Indeed?'

'Molasses, rum and saltpetre. That's the secret. That's what gives it bite.'

'I'm sure.'

'What you have to do is . . .'

'The desk?' interrupted Armstrong.

'Y'mean Jerry's desk? This desk?' Grace tapped the desk with the mouthpiece of his pipe. 'It's as he left it. Locked.'

'All this time?' I was a little surprised.

'It's *his* desk. No need for anybody to go poking around in *his* desk.'

'Do you have a key?' I asked.

'Me? No, it's Jerry's desk, not mine.'

'I,' said Armstrong innocently, 'have a very good screwdriver out in the car.'

'Would you mind?' I asked Grace.

'I dunno.' The mouthpiece of the pipe came into play once more. This time he used it to scratch the side of his jaw as he frowned indecision. 'I don't like messing about with another man's . . .'

'It's more than idle curiosity,' argued Armstrong.

'We are,' I said, 'out for an acquittal.'

'He's innocent. If the law means anything, he'll . . .'

'He'll go to prison,' I interrupted flatly.

'For a barrister you've a poor opinion of courts.'

'You're a medical man,' I countered. 'People die despite treatment. People who *shouldn't* die.'

'True,' he grunted.

'Innocent men go to prison. Not many – I'll grant you that – but Patsold could be one more.'

'All right.' He nodded, grudgingly. 'Force the desk.'

'I want you here,' I said. 'We might need a witness.'

'It wasn't my intention to go anywhere.'

'Good.' I turned to Armstrong and said, 'If you'll provide the screwdriver, please.'

TWENTY

In retrospect . . .

Why force open Patsold's desk? What did we expect to find? What did we even *hope* to find?

We were, you see, clutching at straws. Of Patsold's innocence we had no doubt; Armstrong, myself and now, it seemed, Grace. We each had our own reason for this belief. We were each sure. For myself, I was equally sure of Marty's guilt. Nevertheless . . . why force the desk?

Let us agree that, despite Grace's expressed opinion, I refused to accept the proposition that the police in general, and Leroy in particular, were either fools or incompetents. It followed, therefore, that they had searched the house and – knowing the thoroughness of a police search – it seemed highly improbable that they had missed anything which might have helped either the Prosecution or the Defence. And – again knowing the police – I knew they would have made available anything which might have been of use to the Defence. That they had not done so meant that there had *been* nothing.

Therefore . . . the desk.

Logic suggested that the desk was the last thing Patsold locked prior to his arrest. That it was the last thing he locked prior to the murder of his wife. And – according to Grace – Marty had been with Patsold at the time.

Common sense, therefore, insisted that the desk *had* to be opened.

In fact, the actual operation wasn't easy. I am aware that in novels – especially those which form the bulk of light reading – the task of opening a locked desk, or a locked drawer or even a locked door, is mere child's play. The hero (or the villain) merely inserts something on a par with a nail-file, gives a quick twist of the wrist . . . and the task is completed. Such is not the case. Armstrong's screwdriver was large and made of good, tempered steel. Armstrong himself was no weakling. Nevertheless, the locked desk almost defeated him. It was made of good, English oak and it had been built by some long-dead craftsman. And the lock matched the desk in strength and workmanship. In the end (and much to the unconcealed disgust of Grace) the front edge of the desk was ruined, the woodwork around the lock was splintered and Armstrong had used strong language, but the rollers of the desk could be pushed back in their grooves.

I sat down in the swivel-chair and Armstrong and Grace stood behind me, and we surveyed a desk which was, on the face of it, as ordinary – as commonplace – as the rest of the consulting room. I confess to a feeling of disappointment. What had I expected? I don't know, but *something*. Some book. Some note. Something which shouldn't have *been* there. Just . . . something.

Grace leaned over my shoulder and extended a hand.

'Don't!' I warned. 'Let's just look at it for a few moments. You, especially, doctor. Can you – either of you – see anything even remotely "wrong"?'

Grace withdrew his hand, then said, 'It's untidy. But that's nothing out of the ordinary. The only thing tidy about him is his mind.'

There were, I suppose, two full minutes of silence as we gazed at the jumble of forms, envelopes, ballpoints and general knicknackery used by medical practitioners. It meant nothing. It told us nothing. And, for myself, I began to feel a little foolish.

Grace put a match flame to the bowl of his pipe and again the abominable stench of his so-called 'tobacco' wafted around my head. Armstrong took a step to one side, in order to have a better view of the underside of the various compartments meant to hold envelopes, notepaper and such things.

I raised a hand and, with the nail of my right forefinger, gently pushed aside a blank prescription form which had come adrift from its pad of fellow-forms and the movement revealed a capsule. It was a pink-coloured capsule, about half an inch long and about a quarter of an inch wide. Inside the pink, transparent capsule were pin-head-sized pellets . . . something like those disgusting sweets which, as a child, I'd called 'hundreds and thousands'.

'Lentizol,' growled Grace. 'Jerry was on 'em.'

'A drug?' Armstrong sounded surprised.

'One of the antidepressants. The old vicious circle. He was working his balls off. Which meant there weren't enough hours in the day. Which meant loss of sleep. Which meant anxiety. Which meant he tended towards tetchiness. Which meant he needed something to *help* him work his balls off. He shoved himself on a course of Lentizol . . .'

As Grace was talking, I picked up the capsule and, almost idly, pulled the two halves apart. The tiny pellets – perhaps fifty or so – spilled out on to the surface of the blotting pad. They were slightly off-white in colour with a smattering of brownish-black pellets.

'. . . and *those*,' Grace continued speaking, bent forward and touched one of the brownish-black pellets with the mouthpiece of his pipe, 'are *not* Lentizol.'

'You're sure?' There was a breathlessness about Armstrong's question.

'What might they be?' I, in turn, tried to keep my voice calm.

'Hell knows. But I know what they're *not*.'

'Lentizol?'

'The capsule's been tampered with,' pronounced Grace, with absolute certainty. 'It's *not* as it left the Warner factory.'

'Warner?'

'They make Lentizol. William R. Warner and Co. One of the top manufacturing chemists. Take it from me . . . they *don't* make mistakes.'

I took an envelope from one of the desk compartments. Using the loose prescription form as a scoop, I carefully transferred the tiny pellets, from the blotting pad to the envelope. It needed a steady hand.

Grace complained, 'Those blasted capsule things. Very modern. Very handy. They do away with bad tastes. But why the hell they don't seal 'em in some way, I'll never know. One day some poisoner's going to get the idea. The perfect way of introducing *anything* into somebody's stomach . . . without 'em knowing.'

I sealed the envelope and said, 'Dr Grace, will you

sign across the seal, please. And with the time and date. You, too, Mr Armstrong.'

Grace took a thick-nibbed pen from an inside pocket, then scrawled his name, the time and the date across the seal. He handed the envelope to Armstrong to do the same.

For myself my mind was busy with all probable and possible permutations. Accepting that Patsold was innocent that, in turn, suggested – more than suggested – Webb's guilt. Martin Webb. Marty . . . I can now admit that, in my own mind, I had already accepted his guilt as being established but not proven. Marty was what Grace would have called a 'nut-cracker'. Ergo . . . he handled drugs. Knew about drugs. Was an expert on drugs. Patsold was on a course of Lentizol and – on Marty's own admission to me the previous evening – it had been Marty who had suggested Lentizol. That was one connection. If Edward Patsold was to be believed – and I saw no reason for disbelief – Marty had been having an affair with Patsold's wife. And Patsold's wife had been pregnant when she'd been strangled.

As Armstrong initialled, timed and dated the sealed envelope I said, 'Dr Grace, did you know Elizabeth Patsold was pregnant when she died?'

'Not by Jerry she wasn't.'

'That, of course, we can't say. But the post mortem . . .'

'*I* can say.'

'. . . examination revealed a two-month foetus in her . . .'

'Jerry had a vasectomy about six years ago.'

'Bingo!'

Armstrong breathed the exclamation as he dropped the sealed envelope on to the surface of the desk.

The fall of the envelope brought a sudden, bizarre flash of imagery to my mind. The driving home of a nail A particularly large nail. A nail in the lid of Marty's coffin.

'This vasectomy,' I said in a soft voice. 'It will, of course, be recorded on Patsold's medical record?'

'Naturally,' grunted Grace.

'Thank you.' I indicated the contents of the desk top and said, 'Now . . . anything else worthy of note?'

'The Lentizols.' Grace pointed, with the stem of his pipe.

It was a brown-tinted glass bottle about two inches by two-and-a-half inches by one inch, with a black plastic screw top. Through the darkened glass we could see the pellet-filled capsules.

I tore the top two sheets from the pad of prescription forms and, with great care, I lifted the bottle nearer, and unscrewed the top. Still using the prescription forms as a means of keeping my fingers from the surface of the bottle, I shook a capsule onto the desk top. Then I pulled the two halves apart, and spilled the pin-head pellets on to the blotter. They were all off-white.

Grace said, 'That seems okay.'

I worked with great care. By using the forms, I was able to keep my fingers away from all surfaces. I placed the pellets and the two halves of the capsule into a second envelope. Into a third envelope I shook the remaining capsules, from the bottle. Then, I found a larger envelope and into this I placed the bottle and its screw-cap. I sealed all the envelopes, then handed them to Armstrong and Grace to sign, date and time.

'And now,' I said, 'we need a good analyst.'

'We have one,' said Grace.

'Here? At Pendlebridge?'

'My brother-in-law.' The tone of Grace's voice suggested that little love or admiration was wasted between himself and his brother-in-law. 'He lives here. Works at a manufacturing chemist's at Lessford. Daft in most things, but a good analytical chemist.'

'Speed,' I said, 'is of some importance.'

'He'll be up.' Grace glanced at his watch. 'He's a T.V

bug. The night's viewing doesn't end till the little spot disappears.'

'Will he?' I asked.

'Tonight,' promised Grace grimly.

Armstrong said, 'I'll run him to Lessford . . . when I take Mr Whitehouse back to his hotel.'

'Fine.' I enjoyed a long sigh of relief, then repeated, 'Fine.' Then I said, 'The tampered Lentizol capsule, please. What the dark pellets are. A suggestion . . . some drug used by psychologists and psychiatrists. That should narrow down the field. A report, please. And – if he can – a quick description in layman's language.' I turned to Armstrong and said, 'Another night without sleep, Mr Armstrong. Do you mind?'

'Delighted,' smiled Armstrong.

'Your wife might not be.'

'She'll understand.'

'My apologies to her. Tell her to blame me.'

'For Jerry's sake.'

'Webb,' I said softly. 'That's the only exit . . . via Webb. I need a list of drugs drawn by Webb from the hospital dispensary. They'll be recorded.'

'It'll be in your hand before court opens,' promised Armstrong.

'And you, doctor.' I turned to Grace. 'I may need you as witness. You . . . *and* your brother-in-law.'

'We'll be available,' promised Grace.

'And that's it.' I leaned back in the chair. Suddenly I felt very tired. I said, 'Such a straight case, Armstrong, remember? Diminished Responsibility. A day. Certainly less than two days. Until *you* decided to fight.'

'He's innocent,' said Armstrong.

'When the court *decides* he's innocent.' I smiled a little grimly. 'And that decision rests – it would seem – upon *our* being able to prove Martin Webb's guilt. Not easy, my friend. I know Martin Webb. I've known him a long, long time. His reputation . . . that must be demolished first. And *that* won't be easy. After that . . . his guilt. He's a clever man. Pray that he's made some mistakes. Then pray that we've stumbled across those mistakes. After that . . . pray.'

TWENTY-ONE

I slept little that night. The bed was comfortable enough; the hotel had four-star status and deservedly so. The pre-bed shower worked some of the tautness from my system, but what remained blocked sleep, other than in quick snatches.

My mind was with Armstrong and Grace's brother-in-law. But most of all it was with Marty. By this time I had little doubt but that he was a murderer; that – via some means as yet unknown – he'd killed Elizabeth Patsold and arranged things in such a way as to ensure that Patsold himself would be charged and found guilty. Marty . . . a murderer. It saddened me. Marty, the womaniser. Marty, the lecher. These I could accept. Half a lifetime (plus the charisma which was part of the man) had forced me to accept – yes, even forgive – this monumental weakness in his character. But to *kill*.

And more even than that. From what I had learned – indeed from what Marty himself had told me – Patsold had looked upon him as something not too far removed from a god. It was understandable . . . to me *very* understandable. I, too, had known this near-worship of Marty. This magic possessed by a favoured few which ensures the forgiveness of everything . . . or almost everything. I hadn't known Elizabeth Patsold. Patsold, himself, I had yet to meet. Nevertheless, I would have made a wager. Patsold would have forgiven.

105

To forgive the near-unforgivable. There are men – a handful of men – to whom that gift is offered without real thought. Who accept that gift, as of right. The 'Martin Webbs' of the world.

The thought of destroying him worried me.

The thought of *trying* to destroy him frightened me.

TRIAL

TWENTY-TWO

I suspect that to an actor 'first-night nerves' are a little similar. Certain it is that I know of no successful barrister who, as he (or she) waits in court for the opening of a major case, does not have that slight queasy feeling in the pit of the stomach. I comforted myself with the almost certain knowledge that Clipstone was suffering the same pangs of anxiety; indeed perhaps more so, because *his* witnesses were, in the main, 'professional witnesses' – police and the like – and every prosecuting counsel knows and fears the occasional arrogance and mock-certainty of such witnesses, and how cases can be (and have been) lost by their contemptuous attitude to a cross-examination.

In the robing room Clipstone and I (and Smith-Hopkinson and Abel, junior to Clipstone) had exchanged pleasantries. We all either knew, or knew *of*, each other. We talked of cricket and the County Championship, which was by this time well under way. Clipstone and Abel (it seemed) had travelled north together the previous day (Sunday) and – or so it seemed – had decided upon the final minutiae of the Prosecution on the way.

Smith-Hopkinson had looked a little worried. He was (I knew) a man learned enough in law, but as yet without that all-important knack of outward confidence which at once impresses juries and raises doubt in the mind of the opposition.

I'd tried to counter my junior's worried look by saying, 'Clipstone, old man, on the face of it you seem to have an abundance of eggs. But I doubt if they're all fertile.'

And *that* remark had made Abel frown.

Clipstone had merely chuckled. We knew each other. We knew every move in this game. He'd guessed why I'd made the remark . . . and moreover knew I *knew* he'd guessed.

Belmont, the judge, had called us into his retiring room. The usual thing; he wished to have some broad-based timetable upon which to build an estimate of the various hearings.

'Two days, perhaps?' he'd murmured. 'I understand there's a Not Guilty plea.'

Clipstone had smiled and said, 'Technically Not Guilty, my lord, with a Diminished Responsibility argument, that I take it will be Whitehouse's obvious line of defence.'

'Not Guilty,' I'd said. Then I'd added, 'Diminished Responsibility isn't even contemplated.'

'Indeed?' Belmont had raised surprised eyebrows.

Clipstone, too, had looked taken aback.

Then – with as much confidence as I could put into my voice – I'd said, 'Nevertheless, two days, my lord. Possibly even less . . . I hardly think longer.'

'You have fresh evidence?' Clipstone had asked the question as a corollary to his surprise at my intimation of plea.

'Mr Clipstone,' Belmont had said sternly, 'that is something you must find out in the course of the trial.'

'Of course, my lord. My apologies.'

'There *is* fresh evidence,' I'd agreed somewhat airily. 'There is also – with your lordship's permission – an application I'd like to make to the court before the Prosecution opens.'

Belmont had nodded.

Clipstone had looked intrigued . . . but (as I knew from experience) behind that look his mind had been busy checking and re-checking the strengths and weaknesses of every Prosecution witness.

110

That had been almost half an hour ago and now, in the well of the court, Clipstone and his junior were huddled together talking in low voices and occasionally flipping the stapled sheets from which they must construct the case.

Armstrong and Smith-Hopkinson had joined me. They had been below to the cells and had had a last conversation with Patsold. My first question to them was the obvious one.

'The change of plea. A simple Not Guilty . . . no suggestion of Diminished Responsibility. Does he agree?'

'Yes.' Armstrong nodded. He looked a little grey after a night (*two* nights) without sleep, and yet he was spruce and clean-shaven and there was about him a razor-sharp keenness. An almost bouncy certainty. Had I had time for such emotions, I would have been amazed at the resilience of the man.

Instead, I turned to Smith-Hopkinson and said, 'Patsold?'

'I think he'll make a reliable witness.' My junior knew the information I required, and gave it simply and without embroidery. 'He's a little frightened . . . but not terrified. He isn't bumptious. He won't try to out-smart Clipstone.'

'What does he remember?'

'Nothing. Absolutely nothing.' He paused, then said, 'I believe him.'

Armstrong added, 'That's true, sir. I've been over it with him a dozen times. From leaving the surgery until Leroy found him with his dead wife . . . a complete blank.'

'His wife's pregnancy?'

Smith-Hopkinson said, 'He knows about it. Just about the last thing he remembers. Webb told him about it at the surgery.'

'That she was two months pregnant?'

'Yes.'

'And that he, Webb, was the father?'

'That he *could* be the father. Very apologetic. Odd . . .' Smith-Hopkinson frowned his incomprehension. 'He doesn't seem to hate Webb. Doesn't even seem to *dislike* him . . . despite everything.'

Marty, I thought, dear old Marty. The man with the magic tongue. Unlike Smith-Hopkinson, *I* could understand. Aglaia, Euphrosyne, Thalia – all three Greek goddesses of charm – they served Marty every day of his life; they were his slaves; they ensured complete forgiveness . . . for anything and everything.

Beyond Clipstone one of the court ushers was guiding the chosen jury into its place. Nine men. Three women. For this case a good 'Defence' jury. For a moment I cleared my mind of all other thoughts, and concentrated my attention upon the three women jurors. One of them was doubtful; one of the modern 'glossy magazine' generation; brainwashed into believing that promiscuity was an everyday – even a *natural* – state of affairs. Her clothes, her make-up, her carriage – everything about her – was evidence of her beliefs. She wore her 'modernity' with all the pride and ostentation of chain-mail. She was, however, countered (and, I hoped, more than countered) by the other two women. Ordinary people. Run-of-the-mill people. People slightly intimidated by the thought of jury service. Their male counterparts made up the bulk of the men of the jury. They (the two other women and most of the men) were about to try a man facing a murder charge, but marital unfaithfulness would have *some* effect upon their verdict. If things went wrong – if I failed in the task I was setting myself – then at least (and despite all Belmont may instruct to the contrary) the fact that Elizabeth Patsold had been pregnant, and that Patsold couldn't have been the father, would carry influence likely to affect their verdict.

112

Therefore (hopefully) a 'Defence' jury rather than a 'Prosecution' jury.

'The vasectomy?' I asked.

'Verified,' said Smith-Hopkinson. 'Almost six years ago.'

Armstrong opened his document case and handed me various items. As he did so he said, 'The Lentizol capsules . . . nothing wrong with them.' The capsules were now sealed in a transparent, plastic envelope. 'The doctored pellets. From the capsule we found on the desk. The light-coloured pellets are Lentizol. The dark pellets contain . . .' He took a breath, moistened his lips, then said, 'Dimethyltryptamine. It's one of the hallucinogens used in psychiatry. Laboratory use only.' The pellets and the shell of the capsule were also sealed in a transparent, plastic envelope. 'This . . .' He handed me an ordinary, folded-foolscap-sized envelope. 'Dr Marvin's report.'

'Dr Marvin?'

'Dr Grace's brother-in-law. He did the analysis. He's also included notes on this stuff . . . dimethyltryptamine. Non-technical language as far as possible. And this . . .' He handed me a second similar envelope. 'A photostat copy of the hospital dispensary register for Monday, May sixth. Webb signed for five microgrammes of the stuff.'

'Five microgrammes?'

'Enough to knock out a horse. And, as far as I can gather, there was no occasion to use the stuff at the time.'

TWENTY-THREE

I should have felt elated. I should have felt sure . . . absolutely *sure*. Thanks to Armstrong and the unknown Dr Marvin I had a veritable arsenal of weapons with which to combat the Prosecution. I certainly had enough to insert far more than the required 'reasonable' doubt into the minds of the jury.

Why, then, was I worried?

Why had I a ridiculous feeling that I'd walked into some carefully planned trap? That I'd 'found' only what I'd been meant to find? This drug – this hallucinogen agent, this dimethyltryptamine – there was something wrong that it had been found so easily.

It was a strange state of affairs. Clipstone was perturbed because I'd unearthed something the police had overlooked. Equally, *I* was perturbed because what I had unearthed seemed far too much for mere coincidence. Prosecution and Defence each worried.

I glanced around the well of the court and there, smiling at me from a seat at the back, was Marty . . . and Marty didn't seem at all worried.

But of course (I told myself) why *should* Marty be worried? He hadn't been party to yesterday's enquiries. He knew nothing about the Lentizol capsule we'd found on Patsold's desk. Nor of the fact that we now knew it had contained other pellets than Lentizol pellets. There-fore why *should* he be worried?

Thus the logic.

But logic seemed not to have a place within my thoughts, and those thoughts were such that I performed the ritualistic pantomime required on such occasions automatically . . . almost unconsciously. And only when the clerk of the court said, 'Put up the prisoner,' did I make the effort and cleared my mind enough to concentrate upon the task in hand.

For the first time I saw Gerald Patsold.

A strangely 'small' man. Strictly speaking not particu-larly small in the physical sense – at an estimate I took him to be around the five-foot-seven, five-foot-eight mark – but there was about him a peculiar quality of 'smallness'. Prematurely bald with wispy grey hair forming a crescent from ear-top to ear-top. Clean-shaven; indeed so clean shaven as to give an almost 'plastic' sheen to the skin. His eyes were round, wide and dark, his nose slightly too large, slightly too long and with the hint of bulbousness – I recalled Marty's words: 'Originally Patzold. Spelt with a *z*. A German name. Anglicised.' An East German name, perhaps? From East German Jewish stock? The Jews of East Germany have in the past produced some outstanding medical men . . . few of whom have *looked* outstanding.

The clerk of the court read out the indictment in the approved pompous – one might almost say ponderous – tone.

Patsold lowered his gaze and blinked at the barristers' table. I turned my head slightly and, as his eyes caught mine, I gave a tiny nod of acknowledgement. Perhaps – perhaps it was my imagination but perhaps it was real; I thought I saw some of the fear at the back of those round eyes melt away. Like a small child lost in a crowd who suddenly sees somebody he recognises.

The court clerk asked, 'Gerald Patsold, how do you plead?'

I stood up, faced the judge and said, 'I represent the prisoner, my lord, and the plea is Not Guilty.'

Belmont wrote into his open notebook.

I remained on my feet, then said, 'May it please the court. I have two applications to make before the opening of this case.'

Belmont stared down at me and waited.

'This, my lord.' From the table in front of me I picked up the envelope in which I'd put the brown-tinted bottle from Patsold's desk. I said, 'A pill-bottle, my lord. I request that the police be allowed to examine it for fingerprints and that it, and a report of their findings, be returned to me as exhibits for the Defence.'

'Of course.'

Belmont glanced towards one of the court ushers and

115

the usher stepped forward and took the envelope from my fingers.

'With as little delay as possible, please,' murmured Belmont, then asked, 'And your second application, Mr Whitehouse?'

'That all witnesses in this case be asked to leave the court, my lord.'

Belmont raised surprised eyebrows.

'Professor Webb,' I amplified gently.

A few feet away Clipstone frowned, made as if to stand up, changed his mind and remained seated.

I knew (none better) that I was well within my legal rights. I also knew that this application had never before been made. 'The Spilsbury of The Mind' . . . that was the reputation which had been earned by Marty. And (like the original Spilsbury) his unbiased and absolute honesty in the witness box had earned him the unwritten right to remain in court throughout the whole hearing; like Spilsbury, Webb would never lie, would never embroider the truth, would never be party to a biased presentation of evidence therefore, like Spilsbury, neither justice nor the law would suffer by allowing him the strictly unwarranted privilege of sitting in court and listening to the whole case.

Nevertheless . . .

Belmont looked beyond me to where I knew Marty was still seated.

He said, 'Professor Webb. I must ask you to leave the court. You *are* a Prosecution witness and Mr Whitehouse's quite moderate application must be allowed.'

I heard the sound of movement behind me. I heard Marty's voice say, 'Quite so, my lord.' And much of my trepidation left me. It was a small victory. Possibly not even a victory. Rather, the throwing down of the gauntlet. But even *that* would give Marty some food for thought.

116

I resumed my seat and Clipstone rose to open for the Prosecution.

TWENTY-FOUR

Armstrong, Smith-Hopkinson and I lunched together. The morning had been taken up by Clipstone's opening address and Edward Patsold's evidence in chief. Clipstone (excellent counsel that he was) had done his job well, but without labouring any particular point. Tactics, again, and indeed more than tactics. Counsel for Prosecution is *not* (in theory, at least) an 'advocate'; technically he is neither required or even allowed, to press for a conviction; his task is merely to present the evidence as clearly and as concisely as possible . . . to demolish that fortification of initial innocence behind which the accused stands at the opening of any criminal case. Any pleading – any real advocacy – is the province of the Defence; by counter-evidence if possible and, if not, by cross-examination plus argument, the Counsel for the Defence must re-build that fortification . . . or, if not all of it, enough to create that mystical 'reasonable doubt' in the minds of the jurors.

Thus the theory – thus the textbooks – but in practice (and while no barrister consciously goes *too* far in the matter of fighting for a conviction) the Defence enjoys little if any advantage. In effect (and to equate court-room play with, say, bridge) the Prosecution merely deals the cards, allows the Defence to call the tricks then, via cross-examination and occasionally rebuttal evidence, trumps a way to victory.

Both Armstrong and Smith-Hopkinson knew the practical truth of trial work and, as we lunched at a

117

moderately good restaurant, we exchanged views and opinions.

'Belmont?' said Smith-Hopkinson warily.

'He hasn't come down yet,' I said. 'Neither on our side nor theirs. As the day wears on he may become a little testy . . . *then* his impatience might be used to advantage.'

'He seemed to approve of your objection to Webb staying in court,' said Armstrong.

'My boy.' I smiled. '*All* judges approve of being given the opportunity to demonstrate their power.'

'Nevertheless . . .'

'We'll take Webb when he arrives,' I interrupted. 'What about Edward Patsold?'

'He – er . . .' Armstrong (poor chap) took my interruption as a form of rebuke. I hadn't meant it to be, but there was little enough time, without wasting words on unnecessary apologies. He stammered, 'To me he seemed – er – *uninspired?*'

'An appropriate description.' I nodded and turned to my junior. 'Smith-Hopkinson?'

'He found the body. He found his father. He called the police.' Smith-Hopkinson moved his hands. 'That's all . . . he said it.'

'That,' I agreed, 'is about all he said.'

'I got the impression . . .' began Armstrong.

'Yes?' I encouraged.

'That he wanted to say more.'

'But that Clipstone wouldn't let him? That – at times – the next question followed before the previous answer could be amplified upon?'

'Yes, sir.'

'Clipstone knows his business,' I mused. 'He knows what *we* have to do . . . to move the jury's sympathy towards Patsold. He doesn't want to help us.'

Smith-Hopkinson said, 'But in the cross-examination . . .'

118

'In the cross-examination . . .' Again I interrupted. 'In the cross-examination we have to walk a tight-rope. *I* have to walk a tight-rope. I have to bring out Edward Patsold's emotional involvement – his contempt for his mother – his disgust at the way his father treated his mother, but without allowing him to overstate his case. If he does *that* we lose all the ground we might gain. The sympathy of the jury might turn *against* Patsold.'

Armstrong said, 'There'll be a re-examination, of course. New facts brought to light under cross-examination.'

'Of course.'

'And Clipstone might push Edward Patsold for that overstatement.'

'No doubt,' I sighed. 'Clipstone appreciates our dilemma.'

'Except, sir.' Armstrong smiled. 'He doesn't know we've *seen* the son. Interviewed him. Clipstone's working on guesswork. We're working on known fact.'

'A slight advantage.' The waitress arrived at the table with the coffee. I said, 'Black, please.' When she'd poured for all three of us and left, I repeated, 'As I say . . . a slight advantage. We must try for just the right degree of contempt for his mother. Plus an open admission of *some* disgust for his father. A fine balance. Nothing Clipstone can use as an effective lever.'

TWENTY-FIVE

Which was far easier said than done.

Edward Patsold (credit where due) had smartened himself up. He'd shaved and combed his shoulder-length hair into something approaching tidiness. He

119

wore a collar and tie, a sports jacket and twill slacks. His face was as narrow, as pale and as angry-looking as ever but (during the examination in chief) I'd seen him glance at the dock a few times and his expression had held a peculiar mixture of exasperation and pity.

As I stood up to cross-examine, the hint of a smile – perhaps even a friendly smile – touched is lips.

'Mr Patsold,' I began. 'A few questions in order to allow the jury to visualise the scene. Tuesday, May Seventh. About eight o'clock. You arrived home, you opened the living-room door, you saw the body of your mother, you saw your father. Nobody else was there?'

'Nobody?'

'It was a shock . . . it must have been.'

'Yes. It was a great shock.'

'Your father. Did he say anything? When you opened the door of the living room, I mean.'

'No. He didn't even . . .'

'Did he look up? He was sitting in an armchair, I believe.'

'Yeah. He was sitting in an armchair. He didn't even . . .'

'Did he look up when you entered the living room?'

'No.'

'He didn't look up? He didn't say anything?'

'No, sir. Neither.'

'Was he aware of your presence?' From the corner of my eye, I saw Clipstone make the first movement before rising to his feet to object. It had been worth a try. Nevertheless before Clipstone could speak I said, 'I'm sorry, Mr Patsold. I phrased that last question badly. Obviously, you can't *know* whether your father was aware of your presence. But merely an opinion – your opinion – do you *think* your father was aware of your presence?'

'My lord, I must object.'

Belmont stared down at Clipstone.

120

Clipstone said, 'Whether or not the prisoner was aware of his son's presence at that moment has no bearing upon the case. The witness has already said. His father didn't look up. His father didn't speak. That's all he *can* say.'

Belmont turned his head and stared at me.

'My lord.' I moved my shoulders. I pitched my voice in such a way as to sound puzzled – *amazed* – at Clipstone's objection. 'The witness was first at the scene. The victim was his mother. The accused is his father. I submit that the court *must* know – as far as it is possible to know – the emotional background to this killing. Murder, my lord, it is not committed in a vacuum. Reasons and reactions must also be examined, if we are to arrive at an even approximate truth.'

Belmont nodded slowly.

He said, 'I agree. The objection is overruled.'

Clipstone murmured, 'M'lud,' and sat down.

'Nevertheless,' continued Belmont, 'I think this line of questioning should have certain limits.'

'Quite so, my lord.' I nodded, then turned again to Edward Patsold. 'I repeat the question, Mr Patsold. You entered the room. You saw the body of your mother. You saw your father in the armchair. Do you think he was aware of your presence?'

'He wasn't aware of *anything*,' said Edward Patsold firmly.

'He gave no indication of being aware of anything?'

'He *wasn't* aware of anything. He wasn't even there.'

'A figure of speech, of course,' I smiled.

'Look – sir – my lord . . .' Patsold leaned forward over the witness-box surround. He used his hands to emphasise his words. He looked first at me, then at Belmont, and there was an almost fanatical quality in his tone. 'He – he was dead. Dead! As dead as she was.'

I sat down abruptly. I'd gone as far as I dare.

121

Clipstone rose to re-examine.

He purred, 'Again – as my learned friend put it – a figure of speech?'

'Eh?' Patsold glared.

'A figure of speech,' repeated Clipstone smoothly. 'He wasn't *really* dead . . . was he?'

'He was still alive . . . if that's what you mean.'

'Quite.'

'Still breathing . . . if that's what you mean.'

'Patsold, we are seeking the truth. You say . . .'

'The truth,' rasped Edward Patsold. 'The truth is he was *dead* . . . near enough.'

Clipstone seemed undecided what to say next. Whether to say anything. Whether to continue with the re-examination. He was a fine barrister; whether it was a deliberate dumb-show for the benefit of the jury – whether he was truly at loss for words – nobody could be certain. For whatever reason he stood silent for a moment, then raised one shoulder as if in resignation and, very slowly, sat down.

I was on my feet before Edward Patsold could be dismissed from the witness-box.

I said, 'My lord, might I ask that this witness be required to remain available? I wish to call him as a character witness for the Defence.'

'M'lud!' Clipstone was back on his feet like a jack-in-the-box. The mock outrage could only be admired. 'My learned friend has already cross-examined the . . .'

'On his examination in chief, my lord,' I said gently.

'Nevertheless, I must protest . . .'

'You will,' cut in Belmont icily. 'You will *both* remember that this is a court of law. I am prepared to consider any reasonable application . . . by either counsel for the Prosecution, or counsel for the Defence. What I am *not* prepared to tolerate is counsel squabbling in the well of my court.'

Clipstone said, 'M'lud, with respect . . .'

122

'Sit down, Mr Whitehouse.' Belmont directed his glare at me.

I bowed and resumed my seat.

Belmont switched his glare to Clipstone and said, 'Now . . . you have an objection to make, Mr Clipstone.'

'A Prosecution witness, m'lud. Whatever facts, or opinions, my learned friend required could, surely, have been brought out under cross-examination. I submit that it is wrong – almost outrageous – that, after his evidence for the Prosecution, a witness must then be asked to give evidence for the *Defence*.'

'Mr Whitehouse?' Belmont turned towards me and Clipstone sat down.

'My lord.' It was now *my* turn to play mock amazement. 'A character witness, no more. The son of the accused. Is my learned friend seriously suggesting that because this young man happened – purely by chance – to be first at the scene of this crime that prohibits him from being a character witness of behalf of his own father?'

I remained standing. It was (I admit) a deliberate ploy. Whilever I remained upright strict court usage – and for the moment, Belmont was insisting upon court usage – strict court usage prevented Clipstone from standing . . . and thus prevented him from speaking.

Belmont mused his decision slowly. Ponderously. Deliberately.

'I see no reason – I know of no reason in law – which disallows a man from giving evidence of character on behalf of his own father. Indeed, I think both law and justice would be defeated if such were the case. That the man, by some fluke of chance, happens also to be the witness to his father's presence in the same room as his dead mother – indeed as his murdered mother – does not invalidate that man's right to give character evidence. Law and justice must refute such an invali-

123

dation.' He looked at Clipstone and ended, 'That is my ruling in this matter.'

'M'lud,' sighed Clipstone wearily.

Belmont turned to Edward Patsold and said, 'Patsold you will hold yourself available as a witness for the Defence. Is that understood?'

'Yes, sir.'

'You will remember that you are still under oath. It will be advisable, therefore, that you refrain from discussing either the evidence you have just given, or the evidence you are likely to give for the Defence.' Belmont glanced at the ladies and gentlemen of the press at their table along one side of the court and ended, 'That you refrain from discussing *anything* . . . with *anybody*.'

'Yes, sir.'

TWENTY-SIX

The tricks had been called and to a certain extent the hand had been shown. It had been necessary, but I was under no delusion. As his junior took Leroy through the evidence in chief, Clipstone studied the wodge of statements and documents which made up the case for the Prosecution. Leroy was a good witness; he wasted no words, he spoke slowly – at little more than dictation speed – and he looked directly at the jury as he answered the questions. More than that, he spoke naturally. He refrained from using the jargon of his profession. He 'saw' . . . he did not 'observe'. He 'went' . . . he did not 'proceed'. And throughout the whole of that examination in chief he did not once express an opinion. He dealt in simple facts. He either knew or he didn't know, and if he didn't know he said so.

I almost felt sorry for Smith-Hopkinson when he rose to cross-examine.

A court usher glided closer and handed Armstrong a neat package and a sealed envelope. Armstrong nodded his thanks and slid the package and envelope along the table-top towards me.

Smith-Hopkinson said, 'Just the five words, inspector?'

'Sir?'

' "It must have been me"?'

'Oh, that.' The torn-and-badly-mended lip lifted for a moment in a smile of understanding. 'Yes, sir. I cautioned him – the short caution – before arresting him and that's what he said.'

' "It must have been me"?'

'Yes, sir.'

'And the manner of his saying it?' pressed Smith-Hopkinson.

'Sir?'

'*How* it was said? What emphasis? What meaning?'

'M'lord.' Abel was on his feet. Smith-Hopkinson sat down. Abel continued, 'The witness is being asked to construe the *meaning* of the prisoner's words. An outrageous question, m'lord, surely?'

'Surely,' agreed Belmont flatly. Then to Smith-Hopkinson, 'I cannot allow that question.' He paused, then added, 'You may try to re-phrase it, if you wish.'

Smith-Hopkinson bobbed his head as he stood up – as Abel sat down – and to Leroy said, 'Inspector – as you recall – will you repeat those five words in a manner similar to the way the prisoner spoke them.'

Leroy paused, concentrated for a moment, then said, 'It *must* have been me.'

'The emphasis on the second word?'

'Yes, sir.'

'As if surprised . . . would you say?'

'Shocked.'

'Shocked?'

'When he came to.'

'What does that mean?'

'It took us five minutes – maybe a little longer – to make him understand. He was in the armchair. Not aware of anything. Not aware of anybody. In a sort of . . . coma.'

'M'lord!' Abel was on his feet again.

'Sit down, Mr Abel.' Belmont scowled at Clipstone's junior. 'The inspector is trying to tell the court the truth. The *whole* truth. The word "coma" was his own choice. He was neither led nor encouraged to use that word. The jury are aware that the witness is a police officer. Not a doctor. They will accept his use of that word accordingly.'

'M'lord.' A slightly deflated Abel sank back into his chair.

I'd opened the packet. It held the pill-bottle. I slit open the envelope and read the short note, typed neatly on an official form signed 'E. Nebbit. D/Sgt. 74. Fingerprint Section'. The note read, 'No fingerprints, no smudges, no part-fingerprint on any surface.'

I passed the note to Armstrong.

I felt rather than saw the delight on that young man's face. I certainly heard the delight in his voice.

'It's all happening,' he breathed.

'It would seem so.'

'The odds are shifting, sir. They're shifting fast.'

'Each little fact,' I murmured. 'If we're careful. If we use them well.'

Meanwhile I was concentrating upon Smith-Hopkinson's cross-examination.

'That's all the prisoner said?'

'That's all, sir,' replied Leroy solemnly.

'Just those five words?'

'Yes, sir. Plus the fact that he couldn't remember. Didn't know.'

'Ah!'

'Sir, he was interviewed.' Leroy turned slightly in order that Judge Belmont might perhaps hear better. 'I interviewed him. Nobody else. For an hour . . . thereabouts. I cautioned him. Made sure he fully understood the meaning of the caution. The *full* caution this time. I asked him the normal questions. His full name, his address, his age . . . that sort of thing. He answered. I had the impression that he was in a state of shock, but he answered those questions without difficulty . . .'

(I glanced down the table. Clipstone was scribbling notes on to his foolscap pad.)

'But to every question concerning the murder he said he didn't know. That he couldn't remember.'

'Did you believe him?' asked Smith-Hopkinson.

'That's not my job, sir.' Leroy turned to face the jury once more. 'I ask the questions. I record the answers. I didn't need an admission . . . I had proof enough upon which to charge him. I don't determine his guilt. Or his innocence.'

'Quite.'

(I kept an expressionless face, but nevertheless, I prayed. 'No more,' I prayed. 'Not one question more, along those lines . . . please!')

The outsider – the spectator – always sees the game just that little better than the player. Thus goes the theory and there is much truth in it. It had been a battle of juniors: Abel and the examination in chief, then Smith-Hopkinson and the cross-examination. The examination in chief had been comparatively easy; the police – especially officers of the calibre of Leroy – are the professionals of the witness box; they know the questions likely to be asked, they know the answers they must give. No barrister need 'lead' an experienced police officer through an examination in chief. Like a well-maintained motor car, he need only be started then steered. But when the driver is switched? When the examination in chief becomes the cross-examination? Again . . . the professional is in the witness box. He will not lie; if he has brains, he *dare* not lie . . . of all people *he* knows the consequences of even minor perjury. Nor, indeed, does he need to lie. Ever! He can stick strictly to the truth – the whole truth and nothing but the truth – and still outwit the novice in cross-examination.

And, oh, those novices!

The number of times a good case has been ruined by over-enthusiastic cross-examination. By some would-be Marshall Hall. By some *quasi* Patrick Hastings. By some *soi-disant* Rufus Isaacs.

Therefore, I prayed.

Leroy – honest witness that he was – had earned the confidence and the respect of the jury. Smith-Hopkinson had not undermined that confidence and respect. He *couldn't* undermine it . . . nobody could. At best, he could lay the foundation for the Defence *upon* that confidence. He'd done that. Indeed, he'd done it superbly. But another question – one more question concerning Patsold's manner while in police hands – and *our* credibility would suffer. Our bricks would seem to be without straw. Our case would seem weak and without foundation.

Therefore . . . 'No more'.

Smith-Hopkinson cleared his throat, flipped a page of his notes and said, 'And now, inspector, if we may turn to what might be called the "normal police procedure", following your arrival at the scene.'

It was (I think) at that moment when I decided to present my junior with a scarlet bag at the end of the case; the traditional – and always valued – manner in which a leader acknowledges forensic excellence in his junior. Smith-Hopkinson carried his wig and gown into court in the more common blue bag. At his next case he would, deservedly, carry them in scarlet.

He was saying, '. . . As you so reasonably imply, inspector, this case needed no "detecting" in the more accepted sense of the word.'

'Few murders do, sir.' Leroy smiled. 'Very often a murder is a – er – a "family affair".'

'Quite.' Smith-Hopkinson returned the smile. 'Nevertheless, there are procedures to be followed?'

'Yes, sir. A set pattern.'

'You followed those procedures?'

'Yes, sir.'

'You made a search?'

'Yes, sir.'

'A cursory search? By the nature of things?'

'Rather more than that, sir.'

'You searched the house?'

'Yes.'

'Upstairs? Downstairs?'

'Yes, sir.'

'The bedrooms?'

'Yes, sir.'

'The downstairs rooms? The kitchen? The living room? The garage? The pantry?'

'As I recall we didn't search the garage.'

'But all the others?'

'Yes, sir.'

'The grounds?'

'Oh yes, sir. We searched the grounds.'

'The greenhouse? I understand there's a greenhouse.'

'Yes, sir. There's a greenhouse.'

'Did you search it?'

'No, sir. I didn't think . . .'

'The surgery?'

'No, sir. That's . . .'

'The false roof?'

'Sir?' Leroy was sounding a little flustered.

'The false roof? Surely you searched the false roof.'

'No, sir. We didn't search the false roof.'

'You didn't search the false roof!' The incredulity was, perhaps a little over-played.

'No, sir,' said Leroy flatly.

Smith-Hopkinson murmured, 'Good heavens!' and sat down.

Clipstone almost bounded to his feet to re-examine.

'Inspector,' he said. 'Was there any valid reason why you *should* have searched the false roof?'

'No reason that I know of, sir.'

'All these other places you searched – the house, the grounds – did you find anything, anything at all, which might have added to what you already knew?'

'Nothing, sir. Not a thing.'

'Thank you, inspector. Now, may we turn to the prisoner's somewhat startling loss of memory. He remembered his name, of course?'

'Yes, sir.'

'No problem? No hesitation?'

'No hesitation at all, sir. He knew his own name.'

'His age?'

'He knew that, too.'

'His address? His profession?'

'Yes, sir.'

'No hesitation? He didn't have to think?'

'No, sir. No hesitation.'

'But . . .' Clipstone glanced knowingly at the jury. 'But on matters directly concerning the murder there was this sudden and complete loss of memory?'

'Yes, sir.'

'How convenient.' Clipstone allowed a smile to touch his lips for a moment. Not a triumphant smile. Not a sarcastic smile. But rather a smile which, for that moment, suggested that he and the jury shared a very important secret. Then in a barely audible voice he repeated, 'How very convenient.'

Then he sat down and Leroy left the witness box.

TWENTY-SEVEN

A testimony – and thus a cross-examination – can for the purpose of illustration be taken out of the context of a trial. An examination in chief. A cross-examination. A re-examination. Each has its own form; its own strengths and its own weaknesses. Each has its own basic contour, but that contour alters slightly with each trial and with each witness. The asking of questions – and this includes the choosing of questions and the questions *not* asked – is a craft which at its highest level almost amounts to an art form. And (perhaps) that craft is seen at its best in cross-examination.

Given a liar and cross-examination is easy. The textbooks are thick with instances of great (and sometimes not-so-great) advocates who, merely by encouraging some stupid witness to pile lie upon lie, have demolished the forensic opposition . . . be it Prosecution or Defence.

But given a truthful witness – given a Leroy – and then the subtleties come into play.

Smith-Hopkinson had earned his red bag. Without bullying, without even suggesting that Leroy had told anything other than the unvarnished truth, he had done two very important things. He had established the fact that the surgery had *not* been searched . . . while, at the same time, implanting the idea that the non-search of the surgery was as nothing compared with the non-search of the false roof. He had (as it were) flicked aside a curtain to reveal a possible defence of temporary amnesia; merely a tantalising flick – indeed perhaps an inadvertent flick – but Clipstone had spotted it . . . and, hopefully, we had encouraged the Prosecution to concentrate upon countering a plea we had no intention of pursuing.

By mid-afternoon we were wending our way through the 'expert' witnesses; the tiny links of necessary evidence without which a Prosecution is never complete. Necessary, but even to forensic enthusiasts like myself a little boring.

Dr Grace took the oath, gave evidence of the absence of life before the victim was moved from the scene, then stood down.

Two police photographers swore that they had, indeed, taken the photographs which were then handed to the judge, the jury and the Defence. Black-and-white photographs. Glossy; with each nauseous detail highlighted in order to underline the horror. They included a wide-angled shot of the room, showing the body surrounded by the debris of smashed furniture; close-ups of the strangle-marks on the neck; the so-called 'morgue shot' showing the breasts, head and shoulders of the murdered woman as she lay, naked and pale, on a mortuary slab. There were, perhaps a dozen photographs in all, neatly bound in a grey-covered booklet, with the words 'R.*v.*Patsold' stencilled on the cover . . . as always remarkably like some treasured collection of wedding photographs.

It was late afternoon by this time, and the jury were beginning to wear that dazed, half-asleep-half-awake expression. The photographs jolted them into temporary wakefulness and Clipstone (wily fox that he was) deliberately took them (via the photographers) through each page of the slim album. He asked questions of the police photographers, then turned to the jury and repeated the answers as he turned the pages, one at a time, in order to emphasise the horror.

But when the pathologist stepped into the witness

box to give evidence of his post mortem findings the jury were, once more, relaxed into that semi-soporific state where real concentration is impossible.

As the pathologist droned through his evidence, I thumbed through my small library of textbooks and case books, and as I finished with them, I piled them – not too neatly – at the edge of the table.

Clipstone sat down and I rose to cross-examine.

I said, 'She was pregnant, I believe?'

'Yes, sir.'

I reached across the table towards the post mortem report and ('accidentally', of course!) sent the pile of books clattering on to the floor. In the torpid atmosphere of a weary court it sounded like a shell exploding. It jerked the jurors into instant life. It was meant to. I murmured appropriate (albeit false) apologies, collected the books and re-started my cross-examination.

'The – er – the victim. She was pregnant?'

'Yes, sir. She was pregnant.'

'You found – what was it? – a two-month-old foetus in the womb?'

'I did.' Then the pathologist added, 'I wasn't unduly surprised. She was well within the child-bearing age . . . and she *was* married.'

'Yes, indeed.' I glanced at Patsold. 'She *was* married.'

The pathologist frowned slight non-understanding as I sat down. Then he left the witness box.

The only other witness that first afternoon was the forensic scientist. He gave evidence of nail-scrapings, nail-parings, the sampling and comparing of tiny portions of flesh . . . the final link between the dead woman's nails and Patsold's face, and Patsold's fingers and the dead woman's throat. The manner of telling made it dreary stuff; not at all like the high drama beloved of cinema and TV film-makers. A couple of times I glanced at the jury. Most of them were trying to concentrate, but not *quite* succeeding.

And after the evidence of the forensic scientist came the usual warning to the jury, from Belmont, against either discussing the case or reaching any sort of conclusion before hearing all the evidence.

And that was the end of the first day.

TWENTY-EIGHT

Together we rode the lift, down to the dining room, from our respective bedrooms. Smith-Hopkinson and myself. We had both had a hard day; we had each concentrated our attention upon every possible aspect of the trial. Upon the witnesses, upon Clipstone and Abel, upon Belmont, upon each member of the jury ... and, to a lesser extent, upon Gerald Patsold. Such concentration is a cultivated thing. It requires effort – great mental effort – and was one reason why I had spent the previous night in bed and left the enquiries into the Lentizol capsules to Armstrong. And, after a day of such finely tuned concentration, one feels tired. Very tired.

I once read – I forget where – but I once read that a major court hearing can be compared with a great symphony. The themes, the counter-melodies, the developments, the climaxes, even the movements. There is some truth in this equation. But with this proviso. The orchestra is under the baton first of one conductor, then another. The tempo varies. The interpretations change. There is a constant shifting of emphasis. This is what requires the second-by-second concentration. No case can be compared with some hackneyed, symphonic 'lollypop' in which musicians and audience alike know by heart every note, every pause, every cadence. Each trial is (in effect) a first airing of some

134

new composition, and moreover a composition which is being created as it is being played.

This (although the man-in-the-street rarely appreciates the fact) is why a 'court day' is so much shorter than the normally accepted 'working day'. It is why there seem to be such great gaps of non-activity, between one court term and the next.

It is why Smith-Hopkinson and I spoke very little throughout the meal and, only when we were relaxed in the lounge of the hotel with glasses of watered-down whisky, did we discuss the day's hearing.

Congratulations were called for.

I said, 'Your cross-examination of Leroy was masterly.'

'Thank you.' There was no false modesty. There rarely is in the Bar; every member of an Inn of Court knows what he is aiming for each time he stands up in court . . . and, more, knows when he has failed and knows when he has succeeded.

Smith-Hopkinson said, 'I think the first day's honours were ours . . . slightly.'

'Possibly,' I agreed.

'Belmont was uncommonly tranquil,' he remarked.

'Tomorrow,' I smiled. 'Another day.'

'And tomorrow . . .' Smith-Hopkinson said. 'Tomorrow, Webb.'

'He should be first witness,' I agreed. 'The last Prosecution witness. Unless, of course, they bring in final police evidence of antecedent history.'

'Is that likely?'

I said, 'They try to be fair. He has no previous conviction of crime, but they might feel that also should be emphasised.'

'*Then*, Webb.'

'Webb's cross-examination,' I mused. 'My responsibility, of course. But – as a favour – keep a weather eye on the jury. Let me know. Try to read their expres-

sions. We need them shocked. *Really* shocked . . .
shocked enough to read it on their faces.'
'I think you'll do it.'
'I'll try.' I smiled again. It was perhaps not a very
pleasant smile. In a way the smile of an assassin, ready
to drive a knife into his victim's back. I said, 'In the
beginning a normal, necessary witness. At a guess, the
evidence will be slightly boring . . . even Webb can't
enthuse too much concerning the prisoner's state of
mind. He daren't. Therefore – hopefully – the jury will
be bored. Not *too* bored. A new day. A good night's
sleep. They'll be listening, but without real interest.
Then – come the cross-examination – we should fire
some rockets.'
'We *will* fire some rockets.' Smith-Hopkinson
chuckled.
'With luck,' I murmured.
Then came a period of thoughtful silence. We each
lighted a cigarette and sipped at our drinks. Other
customers entered the lounge and settled into armchairs.
We – Smith-Hopkinson and myself – hardly noticed
them. For some ten minutes (thereabouts) we removed
ourselves from the surroundings and each lived with
his own thoughts.
Mine were a little restless.
I think there is no such thing as complete hatred.
Complete love. There is a balance – in effect twin pans
– and sometimes one pan outweighs the other. No more
than that. That one pan may – indeed sometimes *is*
– weighted enough to last a lifetime. A love – or perhaps
a hatred – which reaches death itself. But (a personal
opinion) such unusual – I almost said 'unnatural' –
weighing down of one pan in relation to the other, is
rare enough to be near-unique. For most of us there is
hatred, there is love and, in the main, there is a mix of
both. A child loves its parents, but loathes certain
hidebound beliefs held by them, and which he (or she)

136

can never share. A woman loves her husband, but detests certain irritating traits in his character. And as we grow older we change and, with that change, the mix of love and hatred changes also. One becomes more, the other becomes less. The balance of the pans see-saws continually. What we raved about last year, we tend to scorn this. The man (the woman) we found attractive ten years ago, we find repulsive today. This kaleidoscope of restless emotion is, I think, one of the fascinations of life itself. Indeed, it can be argued that it *is* life; that only death brings about that pin-point of absolute stability for which we supposedly yearn.

Thus, my thoughts. Thus, my conclusions. And those thoughts and conclusions centred around my feelings for Marty.

The immaculate love/hate relationship. The perfect state of balance; the two pans absolutely level. Therefore tomorrow when I deliberately strove to humiliate him I would (at the same time) be humiliating myself. He would suffer. I would enjoy making him suffer, but at the same time I also would suffer. Equally. His pain would be my pain. His anger would be matched by my own self-disgust. To cross-examine him, as I hoped to cross-examine him, would be a form of self-crucifixion.

I looked around me, saw an ash-tray on a nearby side-table, leaned across and squashed out my cigarette.

'I will not enjoy tomorrow,' I said sadly.

'I know.' Smith-Hopkinson left his chair long enough to squash his cigarette alongside mine. As he re-seated himself he added, 'I have the impression.'

'So obvious?' My smile was a little one-sided.

'You don't *really* dislike him.'

'Oh, but I do. Part of me.'

'I'm sorry.'

'I wish there was an easy explanation,' I sighed.

'You'll do it.' He was a much younger man than I, yet his tone held a paternal quality. 'You'll cross-

137

examine him. With the evidence we have, you'll smash him. Ruin him. And you'll do it – completely – because you're a professional.'

'Quite,' I agreed.

'And *he'll* understand.'

'It's possible.'

'Oh, yes, because *he's* a professional, too.'

TWENTY-NINE

As I'd half-expected Clipstone called police evidence to show Patsold's previously blameless life. A detective sergeant who read from a prepared report and, in effect, said, 'Gerald Patsold may have murdered his wife – we, the police, believe he did – but prior to that crime he was an upright citizen, a good husband and a loving father.' It meant nothing. It was one more forensic ploy. By openly admitting that Patsold was not a regular law-breaker, the Prosecution forced the jury to the conclusion that they (the police) were anxious to credit him with as much respectability as possible, thereby showing that when they gave evidence of evil they should be believed.

No cross-examination was necessary, therefore the detective sergeant left the witness box and Martin Webb was sworn in.

Clipstone led Webb through the necessary 'identity' questions; this minor infringement of the laws of evidence being always allowed. The name, the qualifications, the experience upon which his expertise was based.

Then Clipstone said, 'You have, I believe, visited the prisoner while he has been awaiting trial.'

'I have. On six separate occasions.'

'While he was in prison?'

'Yes.'

'You've spoken to him? Questioned him?'

'At great length.'

'Are you able to tell the court of any conclusions you have reached?'

'Yes, my lord.' Webb turned slightly. He spoke directly to Belmont and the jury. 'In my considered opinion Gerald Patsold is a particularly well-balanced person. He gives no indication whatever of mental instability. He can rationalise as well as any man I know. He is in no way emotionally disturbed. More than that, he shows no sign of recent emotional disturbance.'

Again Webb turned slightly, and faced Clipstone.

Clipstone said, 'A responsible person.'

'Very responsible.'

'By that I mean responsible for his actions?'

'Of course.'

'And his memory. Any suggestion of loss of memory?'

'None that I could find.'

'You spoke to him of this crime? Of the murder of his wife?'

'I did.'

'And his reaction?'

'He claimed not to be able to remember.'

'Claimed?'

Again Webb turned to the judge and jury.

He said, 'My lord, this must be an assessment. Certain tests – long-term tests – were by the nature of things impossible. Nevertheless, there seems no valid reason why Patsold should have suffered even temporary amnesia. An hour's loss of memory. Little more than an hour. And complete loss. Apart from that hour or so his recollection was perfect. He remembered even minor details. I am unable to state, categorically, that

139

he did *not* suffer a temporary loss of memory. But – a personal opinion – it seems highly unlikely.'

'Thank you, Doctor Webb.'

Clipstone sat down.

I rose to cross-examine. The butterflies brought a spasm of mild cramp to my stomach muscles and (an old trick) I leaned forward, stiff-armed and with my hands on the table in front of me, and drew in two – perhaps three – deep breaths before I spoke. I must not hurry (I told myself). Each word – each phrase – must be torn to shreds. Each opinion must be made to seem ridiculous. To pull him – to pull the great Martin Webb – from his pedestal and thereafter demolish him as a witness, then resurrect him as a murderer.

I straightened and said, 'No sign of recent emotional disturbance?'

'That is my considered opinion.'

Our eyes met for the first time. I looked deep into Marty's eyes, and saw the gentle mockery hiding itself behind the expression of sombre objectiveness.

'His wife has been murdered,' I said gently.

He nodded.

'Has she not?' I insisted.

'She has,' he agreed.

'Strangled?'

'Yes.'

'Manual strangulation?'

'Yes.' He nodded once.

'One of the more vile forms of murder?'

'Yes.'

'One of the more horrific forms?'

'Yes. Particularly horrific.'

'Nor are we going back years. Only weeks. To Tuesday, May the seventh . . . a very short time.'

Again he nodded.

Again I insisted upon a verbal answer.

'A very short time?'

140

'A very short time,' he agreed.

'And yet,' I mused, 'my client is – your own words – "a particularly well-balanced person".'

'In my opinion.'

'No indication of mental instability?'

'None that I could find.'

'By that – I presume – you mean no sign of recent trauma?'

'Er...'

'No mental instability, professor. Natural. *Normal.*'

'Normal,' he agreed reluctantly.

'A normal man?'

At this stage it was necessary that I drive the point home again and again. The displeasure of Belmont – the impatience of Clipstone – meant nothing. This was the first wedge via which I must topple Webb from his elevated position.

'A normal man?' I repeated.

'Yes... a normal man,' he conceded.

'You are,' I said gently, 'the Professor of Psychology and Criminal Psychiatry at Lessford University?'

'I am.'

'An authority on the workings of the mind?'

'I claim to be that,' he said carefully.

'Claim?' I jumped at him like a cat pouncing on an escaping mouse.

'Modesty forbids me to...'

'Modesty must not forbid you from telling the truth, Doctor Webb. You are under oath. A man's freedom depends upon everybody – yourself included – telling what they believe to be the truth. I will repeat the question. Are you, or are you not, an authority upon the workings of the human mind?'

'I am,' he said grudgingly.

'Therefore you, of all people, understand what is meant by the word "normality"?'

'I do.'

'These ladies, these gentlemen . . .' I moved a hand to indicate the jury. 'On the face of it they are "normal"?'

'On the face of things. Without carrying out . . .'

'His lordship. The Defence counsel. The ladies and gentlemen in the Press Box. All normal?'

'On the face of things.'

'And the prisoner? Gerald Patsold?'

'That question I can answer with certainty.' We were swordsmen, indulging in a flurry of thrust and parry. 'Gerald Patsold is a normal, responsible human being.'

'Who within weeks – days, perhaps – of his wife's murder showed no emotional disturbance?'

'Unfortunately, I did not . . .'

'A fine husband?'

'That I can't . . .'

'On the evidence of the police. Heard, by the court, this morning. A fine husband?'

'If – er – if they say so.'

'They *do* say so. He loved his wife?'

'I – I can't . . .'

'But *no emotional disturbance*?'

'My lord, I hadn't the . . .'

'He was arrested. He was charged with this particularly foul killing. And he continued to show no emotional disturbance?'

'I repeat, I could find nothing . . .'

'And this,' I snapped, 'is your yardstick of "normality"?'

'M'lord!' Clipstone was on his feet. As I lowered myself on to my chair, Clipstone fumed, 'M'lord, this deliberate badgering of a witness. I must object most strongly. Doctor Webb is not even allowed time to answer the questions.'

Slowly Belmont turned his head and stared at me over his half-moon spectacles. Clipstone sat down. I rose to my feet.

I said, 'My lord, if it pleases you, I will repeat my

last question. I will allow the witness as much time as he wishes in which to answer.'

'I'd be obliged,' murmured Belmont.

I turned to Webb and said, 'To recapitulate, professor. Despite the murder of his wife. Despite the manner of that killing. Despite the fact that he was arrested and charged with that murder. Despite the fact that he loved her. Despite your own expert testimony that the prisoner showed – and presumably still shows – no sign of emotional disturbance. Despite all these things. Do you still stand by your previously expressed opinion that Gerald Patsold is a *normal*, responsible human being?'

THIRTY

Poor Marty. Poor, poor Marty. An affirmative answer meant that his credibility was ruined; 'normality' as measured by the man-in-the-street – as measured by the jurors – insisted that the murder of a spouse *must* cause an emotional upset. Equally a *negative* answer ruined his credibility; it meant that he had either given no thought to his original testimony or that, in the examination in chief, he had committed perjury.

I felt Smith-Hopkinson touch my leg. I bent down on the pretext of sorting through my notes, and my junior breathed, 'He's ruined as a witness.'

But of course.

The fact was (the fact still is) that 'nut-cracking' – to use Grace's expression – was suspect. The state of a man's mind. The odd thing is – and despite the judicial ruling that it is as open to expert proof as the state of his digestive system – the state of a man's mind remains in the realm of mumbo-jumboism as far as ordinary people are concerned. They know, or think they know.

The subject is at once too simple and too complicated. The ordinary man has a mind. He knows how it works, *it* tells him how it works. *It* paces out its own boundaries of normality. *It* – via the imagination – creates boundaries for other minds. What *he* would do, other people would do. What emotion in given circumstances other people would feel, *he* would feel in similar circumstances. So simple. So clear-cut.

And yet psychologists and psychiatrists . . . the experts of the mind. The modern witch-doctors of medicine. They took the simple and made it complicated, but by the same token, the working of a mind *was* complicated. They destroyed established norms, but as the headlines in any scandal sheet showed there was no overall norm, otherwise perversions and outrages would rarely shock.

The easy way out. Dismiss what you can never understand. Scorn the experts with their involved terms of art. Look upon them as charlatans . . . men and women who, in the main, can't even agree amongst themselves.

Any barrister worth his salt can mould his cross-examination of a psychiatrist (or, come to that, of a psychologist) until the unfortunate witness contradicts himself . . . or *seems* to contradict himself. The various nuances of meaning – the sheer precision of each phrase – can be destroyed merely by demanding a generality. The steam-hammer to crack a walnut. The 'ordinary language' – which the jury understands – used to turn the edge of scientific terminology . . . which the jury does *not* understand.

Marty fought back. He explained. He qualified every answer he'd given. He burrowed into a veritable mountain of impossible-to-understand jargon, but the more he thrashed, the tighter the hook embedded itself into his flesh. The jury could not understand, therefore the jury refused to accept.

144

I had, then, discredited him as a witness. My next task was to make him into an out-and-out liar. And in this he helped.

He ended his convoluted answer to my question by turning to Belmont, and saying, 'You must understand, my lord, that these conclusions were arrived at by a mere six visits to Patsold in a holding prison. Of necessity, these few visits could only add up to a superficial examination.'

Then he turned and faced me again.

I kept my expression grim and uncompromising. I gave him a tiny – almost imperceptible – nod. An acknowledgement, perhaps, of a great opponent. And in return his lips moved slightly and the gleam in his eyes shifted a little; it was what *could* have been a smile but, if so, a friendly smile touched with contempt.

I consulted my notes, then said, 'You hold the rank of Professor of Psychology and Criminal Psychiatry at Lessford University?'

'I occupy that chair. I wouldn't call it a rank.'

'I stand corrected. You occupy that *chair*?'

'I do.'

'About a year ago you were in charge of certain extra-mural studies originating from that university?'

'We organise extra-mural on a near-continual basis. We – the university authorities – consider it part of our teaching programme. A vital part.'

'About a year ago,' I insisted. 'A series of evening lectures. *The Psychology of Twentieth-Century Stress* . . . that was the chosen title of the lectures. You, I believe, were the senior lecturer.'

'The only lecturer.'

'I'm obliged,' I smiled.

Tiny muscles at his mouth corners had tightened. That ghost of a smile was disappeared. I was breaking the rules. *Our* rules. I was using information he'd given me in tacitly understood confidence. The information contained within our friendly chat of Saturday evening.

I said, 'Did the prisoner, Patsold, enroll for those lectures?'

'He did.'

'Did he attend?'

'He did.'

'Without consulting a register can you tell the court how many of those evening lectures Patsold attended?'

'All of them. It was a series of twelve lectures. He was present at them all.'

'Twelve lectures?'

'Yes.'

'Weekly?'

'Yes.'

'How long did each lecture last?'

'Two hours . . . thereabouts. We sometimes overran.'

'Twenty-four hours in all?'

He nodded.

'Twenty-four hours in all?' I repeated.

'That's correct. Twelve lectures. Twenty-four hours in all.'

'Therefore,' I said musingly, 'when your evidence suggested that you had only visited the prisoner, Patsold, six times – in the holding prison – when by implication your evidence hinted, *more* than hinted, that that was the sum total of your knowledge of Patsold . . . that wasn't *quite* accurate?'

'I knew him before he committed the murder. Yes.'

'Before he was *arrested* for the murder,' I snapped. 'The decision as to whether he *committed* the murder is not yours to make, professor.'

'My apologies, sir. I meant before he was *arrested*.'

For a moment I stared at him. For that moment I was undecided. The 'sir' in his reply astonished me and, for that moment, I toyed with the possibility that he was using the term as a subtle form of sarcasm. But he wasn't. Marty – the magnificent Marty, who, all his

146

life, had proclaimed and believed himself superior to ordinary mortals and ordinary mores – was indirectly but publicly acknowledging a master. Myself . . . of all people!

It was quite a shock. It silenced me for quite a few seconds and, during that time, I made believe I was consulting my notes as I sought for continued equilibrium.

In retrospect (and much of this story is told in retrospect) my conclusion is that, at that moment, Marty at last realised the truth. That Patsold was my client . . . and that I knew Patsold to be innocent. Further, that armed with that knowledge I was prepared to fight, and cross-examine regardless of all until-then-honoured confidences. That the 'rules' – the 'rules' which, until then, had guided our relationship – no longer applied. I had already broken those 'rules' and – obviously – my intention was to break them again and again, before he stepped from the witness box. I was fighting as he might have fought. As he undoubtedly *would* have fought. To win . . . regardless of the hurt that victory might inflict. Therefore (Marty being Marty) he respected me for it. Respected me and acknowledged me as an unassailable champion.

Nevertheless, I had the wisdom to remain suspicious. If victory was, indeed, within my grasp, I had to inch towards it without allowing my opponent so much as a crack through which he might escape.

I said, 'Twelve evening lectures. Twenty-four hours . . . *before* the murder and before he was arrested. Presumably you grew to know the prisoner?'

'Yes.'

'Well?'

'Yes . . . well.'

'How well?'

'We – er . . . We became friends.'

'Friends?' I emphasised his answer.

147

'Yes. Friends?'

I glanced at the jury with feigned surprise. I was amply satisfied by the expressions I saw on the faces of the jurors.

'We must,' I remarked, 'examine the depth of this friendship you had with Gerald Patsold in some detail. It was, I take it, rather more than the passing friendship – the mere temporary acquaintanceship – of tutor and pupil?'

'More than that,' he agreed.

'You knew he was a practising G.P.?'

'Yes.'

'That as a G.P. he had an interest in mental health?'

'Yes. That was his reason for enrolling. For attending the lectures.'

'You knew that? Or merely assumed it?'

'I knew. He told me that himself.'

'And that was the basis for this friendship?'

'At first.'

'At first?' I raised my eyebrows questioningly.

'We grew to like each other.'

'I see.' I pursed my lips, then said, 'Friends, then. *Professional* friends?'

Marty hesitated, then said, 'Rather more than that.'

'Can the court assume, then, that you saw each other at various times . . . other, that is, than during the lecture periods?'

'Oh, yes.'

'You did?' Again there was false astonishment in my tone.

'Yes, sir.'

'In what circumstances?'

'When he was at Lessford he sometimes visited the university. When I had occasion to pass through – or even near – Pendlebridge I called to see him.'

'Good friends, then?'

'Very good friends.'

148

'I see.' I hitched my gown more firmly across my shoulders, then said, 'Professor Webb, the jury, I am sure, are at a loss as to why evidence of this "good friendship" between yourself and the prisoner has had to be elicited via cross-examination. Why it was not, at least, mentioned during your examination in chief.'

'M'lord . . .' Clipstone straightened from his chair. Some technical objection was on its way, but before it could be voiced, Belmont scowled at the Prosecution counsel.

Belmont almost snarled, 'Mr Clipstone, I too am at a loss as to why this firm friendship was glossed over.'

'I . . .' Clipstone spread his hands. 'M'lord, I am unable to assist the court. The witness . . . What the witness is saying surprises me as much as it surprises any other person in this court.'

Clipstone sat down.

Belmont turned to Marty and growled, 'Doctor Webb, I assure you the court will hang on to every word of your reply.'

THIRTY-ONE

Again, poor Marty. Poor, poor Marty.

It is possible to feel genuinely sorry for a man as you systematically destroy that man. Oh, yes, it is possible. More than possible. Given the right circumstances it is even easy. The great Professor Martin Webb. The charisma was still there; it gleamed in his eye and squared his shoulders; it gave timbre to his voice and what sounded like authority to his words. Without what had gone before he might still have held the jury – held the whole court – in the palm of his hand, but what had gone before *had* gone before, and what was left was an empty, albeit magnificent shell.

Never again would he command his previous respect. Never again would a Prosecution use those broad shoulders as a battering-ram with which to destroy some Defence argument based upon mental instability.

It was, I suppose, the beginning of my own case; the start of that swing of the forensic pendulum whose arc must make Patsold a free man.

The answer was long-winded and obscure. An academic answer which left the jury untouched and unimpressed. His evidence of Patsold's mental state (he insisted) related to a specific period. From the time of his arrest, until the time he stood in the dock. What Patsold had been – how Patsold had behaved – prior to the murder of his wife, had no relevancy. The death of Elizabeth Patsold had been a watershed. Prior to that moment Patsold had been a friend. *After* that moment Patsold had been (in effect) his patient. He (Marty) was a professional; he was capable of complete objectivity; he could – and *had* – closed a door on Patsold as he'd known him, prior to May the seventh, and his evidence (the only evidence of use to the court) had concerned the Patsold he'd known *since* that date.

It was a brave try. My own personal opinion is that had Marty opened his evidence for the Prosecution with this explanation he might have been believed. Indeed, it might have enhanced that evidence. But his deliberate silence concerning his friendship with Patsold was open to only one construction as far as the jury was concerned. The truth – the *whole* truth – that was the oath he'd taken when he'd first stepped into the witness box. And a mere *part* truth wasn't good enough.

I allowed him time – ample time – in which to give his explanation. Again tactics. The more he talked the less the members of the jury would believe. A simple apology *might* have repaired the damage... but I doubt it. Involved, theoretical argument – convoluted explanations – did much harm and no good.

As Marty talked I watched Clipstone. I tried to read the expression on my colleague's face. There was, I was sure, a hint of disgust in the slight tightening of the lips. In the hard sheen of the eyes. The case was slipping from the Prosecution's grasp . . . and the fault was Marty's.

Marty finished his explanation. Belmont's nostrils were dilated above a turned-down mouth; the impression was that a nasty smell had, somehow, invaded his court. I continued my cross-examination.

I said, 'This friendship, then. It had real depth?'

'Oh, yes.'

'Did it extend beyond Patsold himself?'

'I'm sorry...' He looked puzzled.

'Its breadth... as opposed to its depth.'

'I'm sorry, sir. I still don't...'

'You were friendly with Gerald Patsold?' I said patiently.

'Yes. Of course. I've already...'

'He has two daughters. Ruth Patsold. Anne Patsold. Do you know them? Either of them?'

'Of them,' he replied.

'You've never met them? Either of them?'

'I've never met either of them.'

'But Patsold has spoken of them?'

'Yes. Occasionally.'

'In what manner? In what circumstances?'

One more forensic ploy. As with prize-fighters, courtroom cunning demanded a certain amount of feinting. Marty had (figuratively speaking) been knocked to the canvas. He was now upright and (presumably) more wary. My object was to puzzle him. To make him wonder what, exactly, my plan of attack entailed. It necessitated, therefore, my approaching the subject of

151

Elizabeth Patsold via as devious a route as possible. For perhaps ten – perhaps fifteen – minutes I asked him questions concerning Patsold's daughters. Pointless questions, really. But questions which demanded answers. And answers (even unnecessary answers) require the mind to *think* of those answers . . . to the exclusion of other things. What had Patsold told him of his two daughters? Did he know how often the daughters visited their parents? Had he ever seen photographs of them while visiting the Patsold home?

I continued the bombardment until, from my eye corner, I noticed Clipstone lower his notes on to the table and straighten his gown prior to rising.

Then I said, 'Patsold also has a son. Edward Patsold. He has already given evidence in this court. Do you know *him*?'

'I do.'

'Well?'

'No . . . not very well.'

'But better than you know Patsold's daughters?'

'Fractionally better. I've met him.'

'How many times?'

'Three times. Possibly four times. No more.'

'Always with his father?'

Marty nodded.

'Always with his father?' I repeated.

Belmont grumbled, 'The witness will please answer the questions.'

'I'm sorry, my lord.' Marty spoke to the judge.

Clipstone rose to his feet and said, 'M'lord, this line of questioning. We must, of course, allow my learned friend as much leeway as possible in his task of defending the prisoner . . .'

'We not only must. We will,' muttered Belmont.

'. . . but this never-ending probing into family backgrounds.'

'Whitehouse?' Belmont asked.

152

'My lord . . .' I rubbed the nape of my neck meditatively. 'I can only assure the court that this line of questioning has a specific purpose. As will become apparent in due course.'

'It *is* leading somewhere?'

'Yes, my lord.'

'Clipstone?' Belmont turned his head.

'I merely raise the issue, m'lord,' sighed Clipstone. 'I must accept my learned friend's assurance that there is some object in this apparent time-wasting.'

'An object, therefore, no objection?'

'No, m'lord,' said Clipstone heavily and sat down.

'There *is* an object, Whitehouse?'

'Indeed, my lord.'

'Very well. Continue.'

Judicial humour. Heavy and not particularly witty but, nevertheless, judicial humour. From Belmont (that least humorous of judges) and directed against Clipstone. The jury was certainly on my side and now the judge. I could ask for no more. Now it would seem was the time to increase the pressure.

Procedure insisted that I repeat my question.

'Professor Webb, you say you saw Edward Patsold three – possibly four – times. Always with his father present?'

'Yes.'

'You visited the Patsold home?'

'Yes.'

'Often?'

'Fairly often.'

'You knew Elizabeth Patsold? The victim of the murder which is the subject of this trial? Patsold's wife?'

'Of course.'

'You knew her well?'

'Yes.'

'*Very* well?'

153

'Yes . . . very well.'

'Professor Webb . . .' I chose my words with great care. 'In fairness I must warn you that I intend calling witnesses to substantiate any suggestions contained in my next questions.' I paused, then said, 'You visited the Patsold home often?'

'I did.' His voice was low and controlled.

'Sometimes when Patsold was not present?'

'Sometimes.'

'Often?'

'I'd say fairly often.'

'Just you and Elizabeth Patsold?'

'Yes. Just the two of us.'

'An affair developed?'

He didn't reply, but I continued with my next question.

'Sometime – sometime before Tuesday, May the seventh – Elizabeth Patsold told you she was pregnant?'

'She . . . Yes, she . . . She told me she was pregnant.'

'And it was likely – even probable – that you were responsible for her condition?'

'It was possible.'

Behind me – around me – I could hear the build-up of talk and muttering in the court. I ignored it. I concentrated my whole attention upon Marty; held his eyes and kept my voice steady and accusing.

I said, 'Professor Webb, I must put it to you that *you* were the father of this unborn child.'

'I don't know. How can anybody . . . ?'

'That you knew perfectly well that Gerald Patsold could not possibly have been the father.'

'He was . . . He was . . .'

'That Elizabeth Patsold, in fact, told you that her husband had undergone a vasectomy operation some years ago.'

'Yes, she told me that. But . . .'

'That she asked you – *you* of all people – to break the

154

news to her husband that she was pregnant. And that you agreed.'

'If – If I did, it was because . . .'

'And that, in fact, you told Patsold of his wife's condition – *and* the probability that you were responsible for that condition – at his surgery on the evening of Tuesday, May the seventh . . . the date of the murder.'

Belmont brought his gavel down on its block and almost shouted, 'Silence! Silence in court. If I do not have immediate silence I will have this court cleared.'

The noise – and there was much noise – gradually subsided. For myself I felt a curious mix of pride and humility. Never before (and never since) had I caused an uproar in a courtroom. Never before had I toppled a giant. And yet the giant, despite his defeat, retained much of his stature; he stood there in the witness box, moved his head slowly and stared, with open contempt, upon the comparative pygmies whose outraged chatter had greeted the climax of this part of my cross-examination.

Odd, at that moment – in my moment of victory, in *his* moment of undoing – I felt prouder of having known and loved Martin Webb than at any other moment of my life.

I waited. Belmont moved his head in a blanket frown of disapproval which enveloped the whole court, then he turned to Marty and said, 'Webb, you are required to answer counsel's last question. *Did* you tell the prisoner of his wife's condition on the evening of the murder? And – further – *did* you admit to him that *you* might be responsible for that condition?'

'I did, my lord,' said Marty firmly.

'The answer is "Yes" to both questions?'

'Yes, my lord.'

'I see.'

'My lord.'

'Yes?' Belmont gazed at him.

155

'Might I make a statement at this point? On my own behalf?'

'I think not, Webb. Counsel for the Defence has yet to conclude his . . .'

'M'lord,' I interrupted. 'With the court's permission, I am quite prepared to postpone what remains of my cross-examination until the witness has had the opportunity to speak to the court. It is, I know, irregular . . .'

'Very irregular.'

'. . . but with your lordship's permission, might I suggest that what Professor Webb has to say may assist the jury in their subsequent deliberations.'

'It is possible,' said Belmont grudgingly.

He looked at Clipstone, but Clipstone did not even rise to his feet. He merely shrugged and moved his hands in a gesture of helplessness.

Belmont turned to the witness box and said, 'Very well, Webb. In the interest of justice – and in view of Whitehouse's quite magnanimous attitude – you may make a statement. Bearing in mind that you are still on oath. Bearing in mind that, when the cross-examination continues, you may be questioned about the contents of that statement.'

'Thank you, my lord.'

'And now . . .' Belmont pushed back the sleeve of his gown and consulted his watch. It was pure 'Belmont'; a deliberate ignoring of the excellent courtroom clock which showed the exact time and which was directly in line with the judge's chair. He droned, 'We will adjourn for a somewhat early lunch. The hearing will resume at two o'clock.'

156

THIRTY-TWO

I remember very little of that lunch. I ate, I drank, but what I ate and what I drank I cannot recall. My companions were Smith-Hopkinson, Armstrong and Grace. One presumes they talked, one presumes I joined in that talk, but what they said and what *I* said remains a mystery.

I was (and I do know this) . . . I was utterly exhausted. Not merely mentally exhausted; that, too, but also *physically* exhausted. As if I'd just finished some heart-bursting race. As if that morning's session had drained me of all strength.

As, indeed, it had.

I recall – my first real recollection of the meal – that Armstrong remarked, 'Sir, are you unwell?'

'No.' I smiled. 'Tired, that's all. It was quite a morning.'

'We've won,' he said confidently.

'We're *winning*,' I corrected him.

Grace said, 'From what I hear . . .'

'You should be hearing nothing, Doctor Grace,' I warned him. I was, I fear, only half-serious, but what I was saying was no less than the truth. 'That you're here, at this table, could cause comment when I call you into the witness box. Please be advised. Don't discuss the case – any aspects of the case – with either my junior or Armstrong.'

'Point taken,' grinned Grace. 'But I can still hold personal opinions.'

'If you don't voice them,' I agreed.

By this time we'd reached the coffee stage. I drained

my cup, excused myself, then left the restaurant to stroll in the gardens at the rear. I needed air and I needed solitude. The charged and suffocating atmosphere of the courtroom (plus the need to concentrate upon every word spoken, every question asked and every answer given) had brought on a vague, nagging headache; one of those peculiarly incapacitating throbbings within the skull which, while not being much more than an echo of a pain, remained constant. It is, I suspect, the 'industrial disease' of the Bar. I'd suffered it before and I suffered it now. I walked slowly, breathed deeply and tried to rid my mind of what faced me that afternoon.

Marty – the ghost of Marty, the memory of Marty, the residual affection I still felt for Marty – refused me relief. Marty and memories . . . and one memory in particular.

Two days before Marty had called her 'the Pearson girl'. To him she hadn't even been worthy of a complete name. Alice Pearson.

Strange. One reaches a certain age and sometimes romanticism takes over. The past assumes an importance beyond its true value. Had she *really* been so innocent? So delightful? So pretty? The colour of her hair? – brown? – light brown? – dark brown? – auburn? . . . damnation, I couldn't *remember*. Her figure? – slim? – full? – boyish? . . . that too wouldn't come. Her voice? – the subject-matter of our many conversations? – her likes and dislikes? – her hopes and dreams? . . . gone with the rest.

I walked in that garden at the rear of the restaurant and, gradually and painfully, I reached a conclusion. A name . . . that's all I *really* had. A name. Alice Pearson. A girl I'd once kissed. A girl whose hand I'd once held. A girl in whose presence I'd once been supremely happy. A girl – a name – who, over the years, had become a love object.

158

Or had she?

Had she (and her name and her memory) merely been a ready-made excuse? A reason for remaining unmarried? A shadow which I had transformed into a substance to justify my own inability to be at ease with any woman of my own age?

Bachelors. (Spinsters, too, I suspect.) We are the 'odd people'. If, like me, we do not view our so-called 'freedom' as a licence for promiscuity – if we merely wish to live our lives alone with no great yearning to perpetuate the human race – of necessity we are 'wrong'. We ought not to be allowed, because we contribute nothing towards the continuation of society. We therefore (possibly?) seek excuses. We draw back from saying, 'We are alone, but not lonely, and this is the state we desire.' Instead, we weave dreams and invent fantasies. We play mock-martyr. We take some unimportant episode of long ago and use it as a vehicle upon which we might escape our own feelings of guilt, and the accusation of the world.

Alas, Alice Pearson!

Where you are at this moment, whether you remember a lovesick young law student of your university days called Simon Whitehouse, I know not . . . and care less. I wish you well. I hope you are happy. But you served your purpose and, in the quiet of a restaurant garden at Lessford on Tuesday, June the second, I fear you became superfluous. I pushed you aside like the wraith you were. In modern terminology I became 'liberated'. The headache eased, I walked back to the Crown Court with a springier step and the world was a brighter place. Marty and I were friends again – true friends – and nobody fights harder or more savagely than friends!

THIRTY-THREE

Belmont sniffed and said, 'You wish to speak to the court?'

'I do, my lord.' Marty nodded.

'Please do so.'

Marty cleared his throat, squared his shoulders and (as I knew) prepared to charm both judge and jury with his eloquence.

'My lord,' he said, 'I would first ask you – and the court – to take note of my profession. Make allowances for it, perhaps. It is unfortunately, a profession which can never be laid aside. The surgeon can put away his scalpels and for a few hours forget the patient on the operating table. The concert musician can relax in convivial company and for a time forget the difficulties of his next performance. In any other profession a man or a woman can – to use a phrase – "take time off". Not so in psychology. Not so in psychiatry. Our patients are all around us. Every man, every woman, we meet we silently analyse. We do it unconsciously. Subconsciously. Our training is such that we are unable *not* to do it.

'Accept this – understand this – and you will understand my difficulty when asked by the Prosecution to give a clinical assessment of Gerald Patsold's mental state . . . *after* the murder of his wife.

'Y'see . . .' He smiled, spoke directly at the jury and, with a slight movement of the head, motioned towards where Smith-Hopkinson, Armstrong and I were sitting. 'Counsel for the Defence is quite right. I've known Patsold for about a year. I knew him long before

160

his wife was killed. I knew him and respected him. The evening classes . . . that's what brought us together. And from there a genuine friendship developed. But – and I have to admit this – at first part of that friendship was based on professional curiosity. Not later, but at first.

'I ask you to imagine . . .' He began to move his hands a little. Coaxing? Pleading? 'There is a word in common usage. An ugly word. A slang expression in that it has no meaning within the field of either psychology or psychiatry. But there again we have no word *for* this mental state, therefore we must fall back on this ugly-sounding word. "Workoholic". We – the specialists – don't know *why* so very often. And, like all experts, when we find a perfect specimen we tend to grab and refuse to let go. And in Patsold I'd found a perfect specimen of a workoholic. A man killing himself with overwork. A man so addicted to work that – my own estimate – he averaged a twenty-hour day. He never took a holiday. He was prepared to work up to – and even beyond – the point of collapse. *And he couldn't help himself.* He couldn't stop!'

Marty paused, then continued, 'That was the man I knew before the death of his wife. The man I still know. The man I came to look upon as a good friend. The man I *still* look upon as a good friend.

'And the man I was asked to examine while he was in a holding prison.'

Again the smile. Again the tiny movement of the hands. 'I did my best. I did all that was humanly possible. I tried – I tried very hard – to dissociate the Gerald Patsold I knew before the death of his wife, from the Gerald Patsold I was examining *after* the death of his wife. It wasn't easy, but I think I succeeded. Therefore my evidence concerning his mental state relates to his mental state *after* his arrest.'

He turned towards the judge and waited.

Belmont twitched his nose and said, 'Interesting . . .

but academic. And the liaison with Patsold's wife?'

'It – er – happened, my lord.'

'Quite. As did her pregnancy, presumably.'

'Yes, my lord.'

Belmont indulged himself in a slightly theatrical sigh, looked down at me and said, 'Whitehouse?'

'Thank you, my lord.'

I rose to continue my cross-examination. I was, I think, more clear-headed than I'd been for a long time; certainly clearer-headed than I'd been that morning. I had the feeling that Marty sensed the change. He waited and what I can only describe as an approving smile touched his lips.

I said, 'Professor Webb – to remind the jury – you became friendly with the prisoner and, through him, the prisoner's wife. You had an affair with the wife. She became pregnant. She explained that the child couldn't be her husband's – because of a successful vasectomy – and at her request you told the prisoner of his wife's condition, and the fact that *you* might be the father?'

'That is correct.'

'And you broke this news to the prisoner during the evening of Tuesday, May the seventh . . . only hours – if that – before the prisoner's wife was murdered?'

'Yes, sir.' Marty nodded.

'Thank you.' I paused, then with the care (and trepidation) of an elderly lady testing her bathwater I moved into the second phase of the cross-examination. 'As a Crown witness in many cases – as an acknowledged expert on criminal psychiatry – you will be aware of certain basic legal principles built into the English Criminal Law?'

'Yes, sir.'

'The Tolson verdict, for example?'

'Yes, sir. I know the case well.'

'It was taken on appeal to the Court for Crown Cases Reserved . . . was it not?'

162

'It was.'

'And the C.C.C.R. quashed the conviction of the lower court?'

'Yes.'

'Will you please tell the court the reason for the overturning of that lower-court verdict? And how it relates to you and your profession?'

'Yes, sir.' Marty shifted his position and spoke more directly to the jury. 'The Tolson appeal is of great importance to any practitioner in criminal psychology ... or criminal psychiatry. It established the importance of what we call *mens rea* in every criminal case. *Mens rea* meaning a guilty mind. R. *v.* Tolson underlined the irrebuttable presumption that – whether or not the relevant statute makes mention of this guilty state of mind – the criminal law insists that such a state of mind *must* be present before any person can be found guilty of a criminal offence.'

'The guilty mind,' I mused. 'And without that guilt within the mind?'

'No crime, sir.'

'Not even murder?'

'Especially not murder. The "malice aforethought" within the definition of murder relates to that mental condition. In the Tolson appeal – as I recall – Judge Stephen specifically mentions the crime of murder ... and the necessary guilty intent before murder can be committed.'

'My thanks.' I glanced at the frowning Belmont. 'No doubt the learned judge will amplify upon your answer when he sums up.' I picked up the brown-tinted pill-bottle and said, 'This. We found it in Gerald Patsold's desk. At his surgery. Do you recognise it?'

'It's a bottle. Standard size. They're used by the thousand for prescriptions.'

'It was found in Patsold's desk,' I repeated. 'With it – inside it – were found these.'

163

I held up the transparent, plastic envelope containing the Lentizol capsules. One of the ushers stepped forward, took the bottle and the plastic envelope, and handed them both to Marty.

'Those capsules,' I said. 'What are they?'

'Lentizol,' said Marty, having given the contents of the plastic envelope little more than a cursory glance. He added, 'Twenty-five milligrams dosage. White pellets in a size three, all-pink capsule.'

He handed the two items back to the usher who in turn passed them to the clerk of the court, who turned in his chair and handed them to Belmont.

I said, 'Exhibit One and Exhibit Two for the Defence, my lord.'

Belmont stared at the exhibits for a moment, then handed them back to the usher and said, 'Mark them.'

'Yes, my lord.'

The jury were showing an increase of interest. It always is so. Words are ethereal things but produce what is known as 'concrete' evidence – something capable of being *seen* as, in this case, a bottle and capsules – and (or so they feel) they are on more solid ground.

I continued my cross-examination.

'Lentizol,' I said. 'Exactly what *is* Lentizol?'

'A tricyclic antidepressant.'

'Tricyclic?'

'A triple action, sir. It counters depression. At the same time it alleviates anxiety and agitation. The actual drug compound is amitiriptyline hydrochloride. The pellets within the capsule ensure a sustained release throughout a given period.'

'A strong drug, would you say?'

'Not at that dosage. One-hundred-and-fifty milligramme dosages *are* given . . . more often than not in hospital conditions. At that dosage Lentizol *can* bring on drowsiness. But not always.'

'But a mere twenty-five-milligramme capsule?'

'Very mild, sir.'

'What in these days . . .' I moved a hand. 'I think the common parlance is "cooler-downer".'

'One of many,' Marty smiled.

'Was Patsold taking Lentizol?' I asked innocently.

'Yes. On my advice.'

'On *your* advice?'

'He needed it.' Marty was the complete professional by this time. His answers came without hesitation. This was *his* subject, and his tone carried authority. He added, 'He needed something stronger, really. He needed quietening down before he killed himself with overwork. But it had to be done gradually. In a controlled way. Otherwise, he might have cracked up completely.'

'Therefore, you advised Lentizol?'

'Yes.'

'A twenty-five-milligramme dosage. Once a day?'

'Once every twenty-four hours.'

'At what time of the day did you advise him to take the capsule?'

'Early evening, that's the usual time.'

'And on the evening of the murder. You were with him, I believe?'

'Yes.'

'At his surgery?'

'Yes.'

'Did he take his daily Lentizol capsule that evening? In your presence?'

'Yes . . . he did.'

'Did you notice where he kept them? The Lentizol?'

'In a bottle. Like that one.' Marty moved his head to look at Defence Exhibit One on the table between the barristers and the clerk of the court.

'And the bottle. Where was that kept?'

'In the desk.'

'Patsold's rolled-top desk? In his surgery?'

165

'Yes.'

'And having taken the Lentizol capsule what did Patsold do?'

'He – er – he replaced the top of the bottle and returned the bottle to the desk.'

'You saw him do that?'

'Yes. I saw him do that.'

'Do you recall any other bottles in the desk?'

'None. None that I could see.'

'Now . . .' I allowed my mouth to move into a false smile. 'Step at a time, if we may, professor. You saw Patsold return the bottle containing the Lentizols to his desk?'

'Yes.'

'Having taken a capsule?'

'Yes.'

'Then what?'

'It was the end of his surgery. We left.'

'The desk?' I teased.

'Before we left he closed the desk. And locked it.'

'The key? The key to the desk?'

'He returned the key to his pocket.'

'Having locked the desk?'

'Yes.'

'And then?'

'We left the surgery. He got into his car to drive home. I got into *my* car to drive back to Lessford.'

'And so . . .' I moved a finger to indicate Defence Exhibit One. 'When I produce evidence to say that on Sunday evening that particular bottle – containing Lentizol – was found in Patsold's locked desk. When I produce further evidence to say that since he locked that desk on the evening of Tuesday, May the seventh, the desk has not once been opened. When I produce evidence to say that that was the *only* bottle to be found inside that locked desk. What is the only conclusion to be reached?'

166

'That – er – *that* was the bottle.' Marty glanced at Defence Exhibit One.

'The bottle from which Patsold took the Lentizol capsule?'

'Yes.' Marty nodded.

'It has no fingermarks on its surface,' I said gently.

'Oh!'

'Patsold handled it? In your presence?'

'Yes.'

'It has no fingermarks.'

'I'm – I'm sorry, but . . .'

'Did Patsold wipe the bottle clean before he put it back in the desk?'

'No. Of course not. Why should he?'

'Did *you* wipe the bottle clean?'

'In God's name, why should I? He's there in the dock. Ask him. He'll . . .'

'Answer the question, Webb,' droned Belmont.

'I'm sorry, my lord.' Marty sighed deeply. 'No. I did *not* wipe the bottle clean.'

'I will,' I said calmly, 'be asking the prisoner certain questions. I will also be asking Doctor Grace . . . you know Doctor Grace?'

'Patsold's partner. Yes, I know him.'

'I will be asking them both questions, professor, in due course. And one of the things they'll tell us is that for a few moments you were alone in Patsold's surgery. Patsold – and Grace – were both in the dispensary. Can you remember that?'

'Yes. For a minute or two I was alone in the surgery.'

'During which time you could – had you so wished – have wiped the bottle of capsules clean?'

'Look! I didn't . . .'

'You *could* have? Had you so desired?'

'Yes,' said Marty heavily. 'I *could* have . . . had I so desired.'

I glanced down at the table in order to pick up the

167

report from Marvin, the analyst. And alongside the report – slightly overlapping the report – I saw the sheet of foolscap. Unmarked, except for a large and decorated question mark. Smith-Hopkinson tapped the foolscap with a forefinger. Slowly. Gently. I met my junior's eyes, and saw a look of utter incomprehension. That and worry. He moved his shoulders very slightly – hardly at all – but the movement was an extension of the look in his eyes.

And suddenly . . . I almost panicked.

THIRTY-FOUR

It was too easy!

The truth when it hit me, tended to drive all other thoughts from my mind. This case – this murder trial – it was all wrong. It should have been a hard fight – God in heaven, I'd argued for a plea of Diminished Responsibility when I'd first arrived . . . and now it was like picking cherries from a blind woman's basket.

And Marty?

Doctor Martin Webb. The Prosecution's – *any* Prosecution's – star witness. The man I should have feared. The man any barrister might have feared. One of the few men who under cross-examination would *never* break . . . a legendary opponent while in any witness box. And here he was, handing the court evidence of his own guilt with the apparent eagerness of a philanthropist distributing gifts.

There was a trap somewhere. There *had* to be a trap somewhere. And – unless I was already in it – it was waiting to be sprung.

Slowly I straightened. I consulted the analyst's

report, then I cleared my throat before I resumed the questioning.

I said, 'Dimethyltryptamine?'*

'Yes?' Marty seemed to be waiting. Waiting to pounce.

'What is it, professor?' I asked.

'It's a laboratory drug. A drug used in strict clinical conditions. Its more common name is DMT.'

'What *is* it?' I repeated. 'Exactly?'

'It is a chemically structured drug...'

'You mean man-made?'

'Exactly. One of the more powerful hallucinogenics.'

'How powerful?'

'Very powerful. Using mescaline as a base-line, dimethyltryptamine is five – perhaps six – times as powerful.'

'Compared with LSD?'

'Much more powerful. LSD is mild by comparison.'

'This drug – this DMT – is it available?'

'There is a very limited availability. It can't, for example, be prescribed by a G.P. It is not available – it isn't even stocked – by high-street chemists.'

'But it is available at hospitals?'

'Certain hospitals. Not every hospital.'

'Lessford Hospital?'

'Yes.' He nodded slowly. 'We have a psychiatric wing there. Sometimes – very rarely – we use DMT.'

'Your wing?'

'Yes.' His smile was gentle and sad. 'I'm the senior consultant in charge of that psychiatric wing.'

'Now ... in layman's language, if you please, professor.' I paused, took a deep breath and said, 'You

---

* *Author's note*

This drug dimethyltryptamine (DMT) is no fiction. The reader is solemnly warned that it exists, that it is available (albeit with difficulty) on the black-market and that its effects are as here described.

administer that drug – DMT – to an ordinary man. What happens?'

'He goes mad.' The answer was so simple, it was staggering.

'In what way?'

'The – er – the word "psychopath". It is used very freely . . . thanks to Alfred Hitchcock's excellent film. But that's what happens, sir. The mind – the normal mind – does a complete somersault. The capacity to hate is increased a thousandfold. The desire to destroy is uncontrollable.'

'In God's name!' Even Belmont was shocked. 'What do you use this damned drug *for*?'

'My lord.' Marty's voice was sombre. Even sad. 'In our wards we have men – and women – who are not fully alive. Vegetables. They react to nothing. Nothing! Talk to them . . . they don't hear, therefore they don't answer. They have lost all will-power. Even the will to accept the simple fact that they are alive. Our first task – *my* first task – is to establish communication . . . *some* form of communication. To force these unfortunates into acknowledging their own existence and, in so doing, *my* existence. Dimethyltryptamine – in small, controlled doses – forces their mind to work. It produces "movement" . . . of a sort.'

'Hatred?'

'Yes, my lord, hatred. But before it can hate, a mind has to acknowledge. It has to recognise that which it hates.' Again the slow, whimsical smile. 'We can handle hatred, my lord. What we can't handle – what *nobody* can handle – is a mental vacuum.'

And, at that moment, I truly believed the trap had been sprung. That I'd lost the case. Like the magician he was, Marty had won the complete sympathy of the court. The judge, the jury, the reporters, every man and woman in the public gallery . . . like a great tide, the waves of silent emotion seemed to bear down upon the tall, distinguished man in the witness box. He was a god; a god of infinite compassion, therefore he was capable of no wrong.

A witness box. It can be a gallows, but it can also be a throne. I'd seen it happen before. I'd seen counsel – better advocates than I will ever be – defeated, not by facts and not by evidence, but by the sheer personality of some man (or some woman) whose use of words had swayed the court away from the truth.

Belmont cleared his throat. It was a signal for me to resume my questioning.

I pitched my voice a little louder and said, 'DMT, then. This synthetic drug called dimethyltryptamine. A weapon in the armoury of psychiatry?'

'That's exactly what it is, sir,' said Marty.

'But given to a man – a woman – not in dire need of it it produces madness?'

'Yes, sir.'

'Homicidal madness?'

'Just that.'

'The time scale,' I mused. 'Can you give the court any general guide?'

'Yes.' Marty nodded. 'The normal dosage. The effect starts quite suddenly – little or no build-up – between fifteen and thirty minutes. The abnormality lasts for about an hour. Sometimes a little longer, but not much longer.'

'Insanity?'

'In a mentally healthy person complete insanity.'

'And after that? When the effects of the drug wear off?'

'Stunned surprise. Shock. Deep shock. There is no clear memory of what has happened. Sometimes no memory at all. A complete blank.'

'Shock?' I emphasised.

'Deep shock.'

'And while under the influence of DMT, temporary but complete insanity?'

171

'Complete insanity.'

'But *temporary* insanity?'

'The after-effects are shock, sir. But in time – a few hours – the shock wears off.'

'And normality returns?'

'Yes.'

'Sanity – complete sanity – returns?'

'Yes, sir.'

'Now...' I spoke carefully. 'While under the influence of this particularly frightening drug – and remembering your testimony relating to the necessary guilty state of mind as explained by the judges in R. *v.* Tolson – what, in your considered opinion, would be the legal position of a normal, sane person who commits a crime?'

'While under the influence of DMT?'

'His guilt or innocence? In law?'

'He couldn't possibly be guilty,' said Marty without hesitation.

'Why?'

'He would be incapable – utterly incapable – of formulating the necessary *mens rea.*'

'He wouldn't know what he was doing?'

'He would have no idea.'

'He wouldn't know the difference between right and wrong?'

'There wouldn't *be* a difference.'

'Thank you, professor.'

And I meant it. I had retrieved the initiative . . . or, perhaps, Marty had relinquished the initiative. But whichever it was I knew the sympathy of the court was once more swinging towards me. I moved my head in order that I might see how the Prosecution team was reacting. Abel had his head bent scribbling notes. Clipstone was leaning back in his chair scowling his thoughts at the ceiling.

Clipstone (if the truth be told) should have been on his feet half a dozen times. The introduction of the elements of crime as laid down in the Tolson Case was, strictly speaking, well beyond the normal limits of cross-examination and, moreover, I had trespassed (albeit very gingerly) upon the preserves of the judge in encouraging Marty to explain law to the court. More than that, the additional introduction of the drug DMT could, quite validly, have been the subject of a heated objection.

In effect – and via an uninterrupted cross-examination – I had used, and been allowed to use, Marty as my first and major witness for the Defence. I know many judges who would have disallowed my tactics. I know very few prosecuting barristers who would not have fought me every inch of the way.

I was appreciative of my good fortune. I made the most of it.

THIRTY-FIVE

I said, 'You have access to dimethyltryptamine.'

'Limited access,' replied Marty.

'Limited?'

'A limited amount is held in the hospital dispensary. It's an extremely dangerous drug. For simple safety reasons large stocks of it are never allowed to accumulate.'

'But you *do* have access?'

'Of course.'

'And you use it sometimes?'

'Occasionally. Not often.'

'Can you tell the court when you last used this drug?'

'No.' He smiled, and shook his head. 'Some considerable time ago. I can't be more specific than that . . . not without consulting the records.'

'I have a photostat copy of a page of the dispensary record kept at the hospital.' I held up the copy and added, 'Defence Exhibit Three, my lord. If it can be handed to the witness.'

Belmont moved his pen and grunted. One of the ushers stepped forward, took the photostat copy and handed it to Marty.

'It is a copy of a page in the register?' I said.

'Oh yes.' Marty stared at the copy stone-faced.

'The third entry from the top. Will you read out to the court what it relates to?'

'Five microgrammes of the drug dimethyltryptamine.'

'Taken from the dispensary against signature?'

'Yes.'

'Whose signature?'

'Mine,' said Marty softly.

'I'm sorry?' I pretended not to hear.

In a slightly louder voice he said, 'Taken from the dispensary against my signature.'

'It *is* your signature?'

'Yes.'

'And you *did* take five microgrammes of the drug from the dispensary on that date?'

'Yes.' He sighed and in a weary voice repeated, 'Yes, I did.'

'And the date?' I pressed.

'Monday, May the sixth.'

'Monday, May the sixth,' I repeated. 'The day before the murder of Elizabeth Patsold?'

He nodded.

'The day before the murder of Elizabeth Patsold?' I insisted.

'Yes . . . the day before the murder.'

'I'm obliged.' I waved a hand. 'Will you please hand the photostat to his lordship. Then, if he wishes, to the counsel for the Prosecution.'

Clipstone shook his head. Belmont took the copy, studied it, frowned, then returned it to the usher to be marked as Defence Exhibit Three.

As they performed this tiny pantomime, I studied Marty carefully. He'd changed. Despite that moment when, like a Catherine wheel, he'd spun and sparkled round his own subject – when for a few short minutes his simple eloquence had captured the imagination of the court – he was a defeated man. Despite his outward pride he had a strange, trapped-animal look; his eyes flickered more than normal; his mouth was tight and his lips drier than they should have been; his mane of well-groomed hair was a little awry.

The usher marked the exhibit and (or so it seemed) the court waited for the *coup de grâce*.

I held back a sigh and said, 'To clear away any misconceptions. Could Patsold – as a G.P. – have obtained the drug dimethyltryptamine.?'

'No.'

'You sound sure.'

'It is not available other than for hospital use.' He paused, then added, 'I'm told a limited amount – a *very* limited amount – sometimes reaches the street.'

'Illegally?'

'Of course.'

'Are you suggesting . . .'

'No, sir.' He moved an impatient hand. 'I am suggesting nothing. I'm under oath therefore I'm stating the full facts. There is a criminal market for DMT . . . there is a criminal market for *all* drugs. But that is not to suggest that Gerald Patsold used that market. I'm sure he didn't.'

'I'm obliged.' I bobbed my head. 'And, of course, *you* didn't provide him with any of that drug?'

'I did not.'

'Thank you. Now this . . .' I picked up the remaining plastic envelope, took out the two halves of the capsule

175

shell, and handed them to the usher to give to Marty. 'Your observations, please?'

He took the two halves, fitted them together, and said, 'A size three, all-pink capsule. The type of capsule used for Lentizol.'

'Found by me – found by Patsold's solicitor, Armstrong, and Patsold's partner, Grace – in Patsold's desk. *Not* in the bottle. It was not empty at the time. Can you suggest why it should be there?'

'He probably dropped it.' Marty smiled. 'As I recall he took his daily Lentizol while I was there. In the surgery. He shook some into his palm then . . .'

'From the bottle?' I interrupted.

'Yes. He shook some capsules into his palm from the bottle. Eased all, except the one he was going to take back into the bottle, then threw the one he was taking to the back of his throat. Then . . . swallowed it.'

'Returned the top to the bottle, then returned the bottle to the desk?'

'Yes. This one.' He raised the empty capsule an inch or so. 'Presumably it fell clear. Didn't go into the bottle.'

'Presumably,' I agreed. Then I added, 'But no fingermarks on the bottle.'

'I – er – I can't understand that.'

'No?' I smiled. I raised the cellophane envelope. 'The contents of the capsule. The capsule you hold in your hand. The loose capsule we found on the desk top. They've been analysed. I have the report. I can prove what I'm about to say. Lentizol pellets.'

'Of course. It's a . . .'

'But not *all* Lentizol pellets.'

'Oh!'

'Also pellets containing dimethyltryptamine.'

Marty moistened his lips.

'Your observations, please, professor.'

'I . . . What can I say?'

'Indeed,' I mocked. 'What *can* you say?'

Belmont used his gavel to silence the court. Then he said, 'The witness may step down.'

'My lord . . .' I began.

'The court is adjourned for thirty minutes. The two counsel will see me in my retiring room.'

He stood up, turned and strode from the court.

THIRTY-SIX

An angry judge is a particularly dangerous animal. In the past certain giants of the Bar have locked horns with judges and the result has made forensic history. Courtroom battles of magnificent savagery flash like neon signs from the pages of the Law Reports, and the Bench have not always come out best. But (always) the barrister's passion has been based upon a solid foundation of law and fact; always, he has believed in his own cause.

Clipstone didn't.

'The prisoner should never have been charged,' ranted Belmont. 'The police! Great heavens . . . are they ignorant of the basics of Criminal Law?'

'My lord,' said Clipstone wearily, 'on the face of it. His presence at the scene of the crime. The nail scrapings. In fairness, I must point out . . .'

'Superficial enquiries,' snapped Belmont.

'Rather more than that, my lord.'

'You think so? I disagree.'

'They *should* have searched the surgery,' admitted Clipstone.

'Indeed they should.'

'Had they done so . . .'

'Had they done so another man would have stood in the dock.'

'Perhaps.'

'Rather more than "perhaps", I think.' Belmont turned to me and said, 'Whitehouse, I presume you are able to bring evidence – witnesses – to substantiate every implication you made in your cross-examination?'

'Ample witnesses, my lord. A doctor, a solicitor, an analytical chemist. More if necessary.'

'Clipstone?'

Clipstone shrugged and murmured, 'I'm in your lordship's hands. I want no miscarriage of justice. As you no doubt noted, I allowed my learned friend great laxity in his cross-examination. It seemed right that I should... in the circumstances.'

'The circumstances being that the wrong man stands accused.'

'It would seem possible, my lord.'

'Possible?'

'Perhaps rather more than possible, my lord.'

'I shall instruct the jury,' growled Belmont.

'As your lordship pleases.'

'I shall also require a police officer in court. A senior police officer. I desire that the chief constable be informed of my criticism of the manner in which this enquiry has been conducted.'

'I'll see to that personally, my lord.'

Belmont turned to me and said, 'Whitehouse?'

'What can I say, my lord?' I smiled. 'I'm delighted that your lordship has seen fit to...'

'Wrongful arrest?'

'That,' I said, 'is a decision to be made by my client. He may seek advice from his solicitor, of course.'

'And if he asks *you*?'

'I must be guided by how aggrieved he feels.'

'I suppose so.' Belmont scowled, then added, 'But for myself I wouldn't hesitate.'

'Reasonable cause, my lord,' murmured Clipstone.

'Reasonable rubbish!'

THIRTY-SEVEN

But, tetchy though he may have been in the privacy of his retiring room, Belmont knew the Criminal Law. More than that – more important than that – he knew how to reduce the intricacies of that law into bare essentials. He faced the jury and lectured them, like a class of students eager to grasp first principles. He used his folded spectacles as a makeshift pointer and, for perhaps half an hour, he took the case of R. *v.* Patsold and used it as a conduit via which he might instruct the jury as to its only course of action.

'. . . the witness Webb. Whatever you may think of him as a witness I must tell you that, when he explained the law – as laid down by the Court of Crown Cases Reserved in R. *v.* Tolson of 1889 – he was stating a tenet of the law as it remains today. A tenet which has always been at the core of criminal guilt.

'A man must *know* he is committing a crime before he can be *convicted* of committing a crime. In all deliberations concerning guilt or innocence that rule is of prime importance. The state of the accused's mind. The so-called *mens rea*. The guilty state of mind.

'It is said that a man must be held responsible for the natural consequences of his action. And that, also, is true in law. But first he must be capable of *being* responsible. And to be capable of this responsibility, a man must have control of his mind. He must not, for example, be in a state of hypnosis. In such a state his mind would be under the control of another person. Similarly, he must not be sleep-walking. In that case his mind would be under no control at all . . .'

From R. *v.* Tolson he moved to the law relating to insanity.

'... thus, an insane person is incapable of committing crime. The *mens rea* – the necessary control of his own mind – is absent. But insanity in law differs somewhat from insanity when viewed by experts in mental diseases. Medical insanity contains an infinite number of gradations. Legal insanity – the insanity which the law recognises as being sufficient to negate *mens rea* – is comparatively simple. It stems from the M'Naghten Case of 1843. Rules were laid down by the judges, and those rules hold good today.

'They can be stated, thus. In order to be exempt from criminal responsibility on the ground of insanity one of two things must be proven. That, owing to a defect of reason due to a disease of the mind, the accused did not know the nature and quality of his act. Or if he *did* know the nature and quality of that act, he did not know he was doing wrong. Two simple rules, members of the jury. He didn't know what he was doing. Or he did not know that what he was doing was wrong. Nor need that legal insanity be a permanent thing. It might well be – in exceptional circumstances – due to a state of drunkenness. Extreme drunkenness. Or on the other hand it may be due to an intake of drugs. And, unfortunately, insanity resultant upon an overdose of drugs, is these days, a not uncommon occurrence . . .'

From drugs in general, he moved to dimethyltryptamine in particular.

'. . . certain horrific, man-made preparations. We, of the non-medical fraternity, might be excused for doubting the wisdom of creating some of these synthetic drugs. A drug which produces insanity – a drug like dimethyltryptamine – might, to us, seem the ultimate in medical foolhardiness. The necessity for such a drug might, to us, appear unwarranted. That point, however, is not at issue. We must accept the evidence of the witness Webb on these matters. He is an expert witness. Within the field of his expertise, he has not been

180

challenged. We must, therefore, accept his opinion in that field without qualification.

'In so doing, however, we must accept his reply to the question relating to the effect of dimethyltryptamine when administered to sane persons. The answer was quite categorical. It drives them mad. Until the effects of that drug wear off they are insane . . .'

Then Belmont turned to the evidence. With a periodic glance at his notes, he took the jury through the whole case for the Prosecution, witness at a time.

'. . . the witness Edward Patsold. He was first on the scene of this crime. He saw evidence of a fight. A struggle. He saw his dead mother. He saw the prisoner . . . his father. The prisoner was in an armchair. To use Edward Patsold's own expression . . . the prisoner was as "dead" as she was. An exaggeration, of course. But, taking it as a figure of speech, both graphic and illuminating . . .

'. . . especially is Edward Patsold's evidence of importance when taken in conjunction with the evidence of the police witness, Leroy. The prisoner was still in "a sort of coma" when the police arrived at the scene, after being sent for by Edward Patsold. The words. "It *must* have been me." Neither an admission, nor a denial. But, you might think, a remark consistent with a man just recovering from drug-induced insanity. And despite police questioning a complete blank, as far as the murder itself is concerned. A puzzling remark – a puzzling loss of memory – until we remember the effect of the drug dimethyltryptamine.

'Which brings me to a criticism. A major criticism of the manner in which the police handled this enquiry. It is my considered opinion that they took too much for granted. They forgot their first duty. The collection of evidence. All evidence. For, and against. Had they done their duty they would have searched the surgery. They would have searched the desk. They would have found

181

the bottle containing the Lentizol capsules. They would have examined that bottle for fingerprints. They would have found the loose capsule containing pellets which included the drug dimethyltryptamine. There was, in my opinion, a gross neglect of duty on the part of the police. And, you might think, had they performed their duty adequately the prisoner, Patsold, would not be before us in this court...

'. . . the scientific evidence, relating to nail-scrapings and portions of flesh, which link the prisoner's fingers with the neck of his dead wife and *her* fingers with the claw-marks found on Patsold's face. Conclusive evidence which was not challenged. But that evidence does not stand alone. It must not be taken out of the context of the cross-examination of other witnesses. The manner of the prisoner when found at the scene. The drug, dimethyltryptamine, and its effect upon a sane person. The fact that that drug was found in the prisoner's desk disguised as a Lentizol capsule. The cross-examination, ladies and gentlemen of the jury. That, too, is evidence. And it might be that the evidence brought forth in cross-examination tends to invalidate the natural conclusions drawn from the presence of flesh beneath the fingernails of both the prisoner and the dead woman...

'. . . the witness, Webb. At first an evasive witness. Thereafter, a strangely honest witness. In his evidence in chief he made no mention of knowing the prisoner prior to the commission of this crime. Then under cross-examination he openly admitted friendship – great friendship – with Patsold. And an even greater friendship with the dead woman. A friendship which amounted to an affair. And, as a result of that affair, the possibility that he was the father of the dead woman's unborn child.

'Now, members of the jury, I must say a few words upon the subject of motive. The Defence have put forward no motive for this crime. Nor need they do so.

Crimes are committed for a multiplicity of motives and, sometimes, the motive is unknown. That a murder is committed is enough. *Why* it is committed is of secondary importance.

'Nevertheless motive, when it is proved – when it is implied – must have a place within the considerations of a criminal court. And the pregnancy of a wife whose husband has undergone a vasectomy must be viewed as a possible motive. A motive on the part of the husband. But, also, a motive on the part of the man responsible for that woman's condition . . . especially if that man enjoys some professional standing in the community.

'Other things must be taken into consideration, also. The fact that the prisoner was undergoing a course of Lentizol on the advice of the witness Webb. That Webb visited the prisoner at the surgery on the evening of the murder. That Webb told the prisoner of his wife's condition. That a Lentizol capsule was found at that same surgery and that Lentizol capsule contained the drug dimethyltryptamine. That this drug is difficult to obtain, but that Webb is one of the few people able to obtain it. That, in fact, he *did* obtain it – five microgrammes of the drug – against his signature on the day before the murder. That the bottle containing the Lentizol capsules had no fingermarks on it . . . even though Webb admits to seeing the prisoner handle that bottle. Why? Because it was wiped clean? And if it was wiped clean, *why* was it wiped clean?

'These questions – the whole of the evidence for the Defence – add up to certain conclusions. Conclusions which, hopefully, the police will take note of. But as far as this court is concerned, conclusions which amount to doubt. Considerable doubt . . .'

Finally, Belmont explained the law relating to criminal responsibility.

'. . . the case of Woolmington *v.* The Director of

Public Prosecutions. This case was heard in 1935. It was taken to the House of Lords, and once and for all, the ground rules were laid. What I have already mentioned – the *mens rea* – was explained in detail. And it was agreed, the onus of proving beyond reasonable doubt that the accused committed the guilty act was insufficient. The Prosecution, it was agreed, must also prove the guilty mind requisite for the crime. That this guilty mind must *never* be presumed from the fact that the accused committed a guilty act.

'It was said – and every judge must agree – that throughout the web of the English Criminal Law one golden thread is always to be seen. And that web is the duty of the Prosecution to prove the guilt of the prisoner beyond all reasonable doubt. Which means that at the end of a criminal hearing if, as a result of evidence given by the Prosecution or the Defence – by either examination or cross-examination – there is reasonable doubt as to whether the accused had malicious intention the Prosecution has failed. The accused is entitled to an acquittal.

'You have heard the evidence called by the Prosecution. You have heard much – indeed *most* – of that evidence countered and demolished by cross-examination. Much more than the required "reasonable doubt" has been introduced into this hearing. *Much* more. Indeed, had the police carried out their duties in a conscientious manner, the certainty is that a lower court would not have committed Patsold to this court for trial. I will go further. It is my considered opinion that a charge of Wrongful Arrest might well be based upon the manner in which the police carried out this enquiry.

'I must tell you, therefore, that clear doubt has been established as to the guilt of the prisoner, and that doubt can but be increased should the Defence bring forward more witnesses and more evidence. Massive

184

doubt – doubt almost amounting to certainty – has come from the mouths of witnesses giving evidence for the Prosecution. And for that reason I have taken this unusual, but not unique, step of interrupting the course of this trial in order to instruct you as to your only course of action. In law, much less fact, the degree of doubt, which *must* be granted to Gerald Patsold, has been more than established. An acquittal is the only verdict open to you. I ask you, therefore, ladies and gentlemen of the jury, to retire if you wish but, whether or not you retire, I must instruct you to bring in a verdict of Not Guilty.'

He paused, then looked directly at Clipstone and ended, 'I also wish my surprise and annoyance to be recorded. A surprise and an annoyance that the valuable time of this court, and of the members of the jury, should have been wasted by the bringing of this frivolous charge.'

The jury did not retire. They leaned forward and sideways and, after muttered consultations, delivered their verdict.

And fifteen minutes later Gerald Patsold walked the streets of Lessford a free man.

THIRTY-EIGHT

That evening Smith-Hopkinson and I took the train south. It was Tuesday, July the second, and as we watched the cloudscape from the dining-car window, the reds, the golds, the yellows, the blues and the greens gave promise of a hot high-summer. We were both strangely silent . . . each, perhaps, for his own reason.

For myself, I was sad. Sad that, at last, having rid myself of the ghost of a lost love who (when faced with the cold hard beam of logic) had been no love at all, I could have enjoyed the friendship – the *genuine* friendship – of Marty. Could have enjoyed that friendship, had I not been obliged to destroy that friendship in the cause of Gerald Patsold.

Not for the first time I allowed my mind to dwell upon the disadvantages of my chosen profession. A barrister-at-law . . . that above all else. An advocate. A pleader and often a pleader of lost causes. A man paid to fight other men's battles. And if in that fight his own life becomes ,less complete . . . what of it? A wig, a gown and a voice. Beyond that, nothing. A repository of legal ploys and courtroom tactics. A man learned in the ways of his fellows; learned in the weaknesses of witnesses; learned in the likes and dislikes of judges; learned in the sometimes lunatic decisions of juries.

A strange profession.

Perhaps, after all, not a particularly honourable profession . . .

POST-TRIAL

THIRTY-NINE

At that point it was a case; one of many interesting briefs; interesting enough to merit the telling in convivial and forensically minded company, but in no way unique. On a personal level it was my first appearance for the Defence in which the judge had stopped the hearing before the trial had ended. That of itself was worth an occasional dusty chuckle within the somewhat dry atmosphere of the Inns and their environs. But no more than that.

As for my soul-searching on my journey south from Lessford, that was very short-lived. I was part of a busy chambers, and each day saw some new and subtle obscurity superimposed upon one of the limited legal puzzles. My life was my work. My work was (to me) fascinating. Ergo . . . my life was far too interesting to admit of either boredom or self-recrimination.

As I had promised myself I presented Smith-Hopkinson with a deserved red bag and (as expected) the recipient expressed mock surprise. He entertained every member of the chambers to a celebratory supper . . . and that, I think, gave him as much pleasure as did the scarlet carrier for his court attire.

For the rest it was a quiet and comparatively sober existence. For a time I half-expected some form of communication from Armstrong concerning the advisability or otherwise of pursuing the matter of Wrongful Arrest. I think I would have advised against. We had been lucky – or, to be strictly accurate, Gerald Patsold had been lucky. Had that single Lentizol capsule not spilled from his hand and on to the desk instead of into the bottle, any barrister would have been hard pressed to obtain any verdict other than Murder reduced to Manslaughter on a plea of Diminished Responsibility. But the request for advice never came, and I assumed that either the matter had not been pressed or, if it had been pressed, Armstrong had (rightly) thought himself a competent enough lawyer not to need counsel's opinion. And gradually – like papers left in some 'Pending' file – the case of R. *v.* Patsold became overlaid with other cases of equal interest. It was (if you recall) a blazing July. London seemed to shimmer as if under a giant burning glass. Secretaries and other office workers filled every green space each lunch time with their sandwiches and cold drinks. And when it wasn't secretaries, it was sun-worshippers, stripped as far as the law would allow, stretched out to catch the ultra-violet and the infra-red, like so many deformed steaks under a grid. And at Lord's the great summer game was played as it should be played; as it is so rarely played; with cunning and fury on a hard-baked pitch, and played for a win and not for a draw, with the white against the green under a duck-egg blue sky and the face of the bat showing scarlet bruise marks as proof of full-blooded drives.

It was a glorious July and, although I was obliged to spend most of the month cooped up in chambers or listening to some dreary tale of misfortune in a stuffy court, I nevertheless felt the warmth soak into my ageing bones . . . and for a few golden days I almost felt the return of youth.

That July was my undoing. It played tricks on me. I had arranged to take a fortnight's holiday from the third to the seventeenth of August; my usual break in the quiet of the Dorset countryside not far from Lyme Regis. Instead I ended in Suffolk assisting my only nephew – a young and enthusiastic architect whose hobby seemed to be dismembering broken-down barns and resurrecting them as 'much sought after' country dwellings – assisting him in the final stages of interior decoration. It seemed a good idea. He and I got along splendidly together. The July sun had made me feel younger than my age, and a short spell of mild physical exercise seemed not merely pleasant, but positively necessary.

In the event, the heavens opened on the Friday – August the second – and the following day I arrived at my Suffolk destination tired, more than a little wet and already regretting my change of plans.

By the Sunday evening I was in a brighter mood, thanks to an out-of-season log fire, a liberal supply of good whisky, some fine music on an excellent hi-fi record player and the easy conviviality of my nephew. His latest masterpiece was (it must be admitted) bordering upon the miraculous. What had been an unused byre was now a 'place in the country' ready to be snapped up by any prowling member of the *nouveaux riches*. The structural alterations were finished. All the ground floor rooms had been decorated, as had two of the bedrooms and both bathrooms. Only the two guest bedrooms now needed finishing off.

That evening (the Sunday) we sprawled in second-hand (albeit, surprisingly comfortable) armchairs and exchanged small-talk about this, his latest venture.

'It could become a full-time occupation,' he smiled.

'A gamble . . . surely?' I tasted fine whisky.

'Mugs with money, Simon.' He was of the generation used to addressing even elder members of the family – even his own parents – on a first-name basis. At first, it had seemed slightly tasteless, but with usage it had become acceptable. Even pleasant. It gave one a feeling of being wanted, for oneself and not out of a sense of duty. He said, 'They're a rootless crowd. They "invest". With them it's almost a religion.'

'And they invest in these places?'

'Bricks an' mortar, lad.' His mock North Country

accent was a delightful, unbarbed mockery. 'There's nowt like bricks an' mortar.'

'They could have a point.'

'Oh, they *have*.' Again that sudden, artless smile. 'That's what I'm doing . . . in effect.'

'Ah, yes. But you're putting something of yourself into each of these conversions.'

'And I don't come cheap,' he chuckled.

'Nevertheless . . .'

'Simon. The *hoi polloi*. Give them money – large amounts of money – and they don't know what the devil to do with it. It scares 'em. They retain a weekly-wage-packet mentality. What they can't handle – what they can't actually *see*, what they can't dump on a table and count – they don't understand. A place like this . . .' He waved a languid hand. 'They've read. They've seen photographs in the county magazines. Hovels turned into picture-postcard houses. Miles from anywhere. They all fancy the role of landed gentry, but without the mess and muck of actually farming. *This* is what they're after. On back-slapping terms with the local vicar. Maybe some hack novelist lives hereabouts . . . somebody to booze with at the local. All these things help.'

'You're a cynic,' I said.

'Certainly. It pays.' He sipped whisky. 'It's been going on for years. Somerset, Hampshire, Sussex, Kent – all the Southern counties – there isn't a barn, there isn't an outhouse left. They've all had the old face-lift. Now we're moving north. Suffolk, Norfolk. On the west side Shropshire. Some of my pals are already winkling out poverty-stricken dumps in Lincolnshire. And why not? This place . . .' Again he moved a hand. 'If I don't make four-hundred-per-cent clear profit on this little heap of stones, I've lost my touch.'

'You are also,' I observed, 'something of a smart operator.'

192

'Of course. But within the law.'

'Of course,' I agreed. 'Otherwise *I* wouldn't be here.'

And thus that pleasant Sunday evening passed. There was no 'generation gap'. Instead, there was an exchange of simple honesty with, occasionally, a break in which we remained silent and listened to the soothing music of Bach or Mozart.

It was almost midnight when we retired and, despite the slight make-do-and-mend furnishings installed as a temporary measure, I slept deeply and without dreams. It had (I decided, as I closed my eyes) been a good idea, after all. A pleasant change. An unusual, but nevertheless a promising holiday . . . to be a tiny part of a creation.

FORTY

In fact, it was *not a* good idea. It was a monumentally *bad* idea. It stopped being a good idea – became an idiotic idea – at about ten minutes after eleven o'clock the next morning.

The original adze-hewn beams had been left in the guest bedroom. Proud and seasoned beams of English oak; cleaned and treated against the myriad ailments which can ruin good wood, and thus darkened, as if fumed. The mush between these beams had been stripped to the stonework and thereafter plasterwork had formed a background from which these magnificent beams had stood out like a gigantic framework in the sloping ceiling. Top quality emulsion paint – ivory coloured – had been applied to the plaster. Three coats already, and already the contrast of almost-black against almost-white gave the room a stark beauty which (hopefully) would hypnotise prospective buyers into parting with money.

My task was to apply a fourth and final coat of emulsion paint to the plaster.

'And the wood, Simon. Take your time. No rush. Just cover all the plaster, but keep it off the beams. It's hell's own job shifting it from the grain if you make a mistake.'

Thus my working instructions and, as I shuffled along the planks which bridged the two stepladders, I was conscious of my responsibility. A moment's lack of concentration and perfection would become marred.

I bent my head to catch the reflection of the sun through the window and on to the paintwork. It was difficult – almost impossible – to see where I'd already painted and where I had yet to paint. I backed away slightly in order to get a better view. My heel slipped from the edge of the plank. I threw myself forward and, at the same time, clutched at the paint and the brush, twisting myself in order not to have a spillage; in order not to allow the paint-soaked bristles to touch those precious beams. For a moment every ounce of my threshing body was balanced on the ball of my left foot on the edge of the plank.

I think I heard it first. I think I heard it, before I actually felt it. It sounded like the snapping of thick, strong elastic. But having heard it, I *then* felt it.

Later (in hospital) I was told that the snapping of the Achilles' tendon, is momentarily, far more painful than the breaking of a bone. I have no reason at all to doubt that statement. Certain it is that *I* had never before felt such pain. For one mad moment I seriously thought my foot had snapped off at the ankle. I ended up on the bedroom floor, soaked in ivory-coloured emulsion paint, clasping my left foot, just above the heel, gasping and quite unable to speak because of the excruciating agony.

FORTY-ONE

Nor was the orthopaedic surgeon a man of infinite optimism.

He eyed my bound and plastered lower limb and said, 'Six weeks. At least six weeks, then we'll try you on crutches.'

'In heaven's name!' I protested. 'I've snapped a ligament, that's all.'

'*The* ligament.' He scowled his disapproval at my protestations. 'It used to be called ham-stringing. The Japs used it on the Burmese Railway. Any attempt at escape, they sliced the ham-string. The poor devil couldn't walk – much less run away – after that. They're still around. Men with limps. They'll limp for the rest of their lives.'

'This is Lowestoft . . . not the Burmese jungle.'

'It's a good nursing home,' he agreed. 'One of the best. *And* I know my job. But if you rush things, you'll end up with internal scar tissue . . . and a limp. It's your decision. You're paying.'

'A limp?' I muttered.

'Less than six weeks on your back . . . I'll guarantee it. *And* you'll know when rain's on the way. You'll have toothache all around your ankle.'

Behind him the nurse tried to suppress a smile. She was young, pretty, on the threshold of life. It amused her to see and hear two middle-aged-to-elderly men being politely rude to each other.

I said, 'When can I move from here?'

'I've already told you. Six . . .'

'Motor cars – even ambulances – *have* been invented.'

'Oh!'

195

'I have a flat in London.'

'I'd like you here for a fortnight,' he said. 'Any complications... they'll show by then.'

'Then I can go home?'

'Hopefully.' He moved his hands despairingly. 'Why you should choose London when you can stay on here at Lowestoft...'

But I did, and was glad to get back there.

Not, let me hasten to add, that the Lowestoft nursing home could be seriously faulted. I enjoyed all the attention I needed; at times more attention than I felt like. The meals were good ... even imaginative. And a broken foot had no effect upon my appetite. The pretty young nurse seemed to look upon me as her personal responsibility. She spoiled me outrageously; she even smuggled a bottle of whisky into the tiny, private ward ... on the strict understanding, of course, that should it be found she *hadn't*. But it was a very boring fortnight. The TV set at the foot of my bed, catered for a general level of near-moronic intelligence; that or some pompous ass talked *at* me in terms well beyond my comprehension. Nor was the radio above my head much better. It was either the incomprehensible cacophony of so-called 'pop', or the (to me) equally cacophonic ramblings of 'modern' classical music. I promised myself the pleasure of penning a stiff letter of complaint to the B.B.C. when I arrived home.

My little nurse did her best. I asked for books ... and she brought me books. But what books! From some local lending library she unearthed what purported to be 'light reading' ... a euphemism, it would seem, for the dreary – monotonous – description of copulation within a series of near-impossible situations. I hadn't the heart to complain. She tried so hard to please and (one must presume) this particular brand of literary garbage was what she considered appropriate reading matter.

196

Noel (my nephew) visited me a couple of times. Each time he was most congratulatory. Despite my tumble – despite the pain – I had not, it seemed, so much as spotted his beloved beams with emulsion paint. He was very grateful.

'One tries to please,' I murmured.

'Fantastic how you clung on to that pot of paint and that brush until you were well clear of the wall and ceiling.'

'A reflex action, I assure you.'

'If I can do anything to show my appreciation . . .'

'You can drive me home.'

'Surely.'

'On August nineteenth. Monday.'

'I thought the quack said . . .'

'He seems to think Lowestoft is the hallway to paradise. It isn't. Not from here. I wish to go home.'

'Okay.' Noel grinned.

'Something – some vehicle – which doesn't necessitate my foot touching the ground.'

'A shooting-brake?' he suggested.

'That, I think, would be ideal.'

And it was. Cocooned in pillows and blankets, with the back of the front passenger's seat as a headrest, it was a remarkably pleasant journey. My friend, the orthopaedic surgeon, telephoned my own medic, giving an approximate time of arrival and, by the time Noel and London-based friends (my nephew is of a generation capable of producing 'friends' at every road junction) . . . by the time Noel and friends had literally lifted me from the shooting-brake, and carried me into the flat to instal me in my own bed, James (my own G.P.) had arrived and was fussing around, as if it was my neck and not my foot which had been broken.

197

FORTY-TWO

For some weeks (my diary tells me until September the fourteenth) I led a comfortable, if boring life. James called in each day, usually after his rounds, and stayed for an hour or two to discuss the current lunacy of national and international politics. I read a great deal and, for the umpteenth time, marvelled that men with great wisdom (like Dicey, Maitland and Jennings) could disagree so widely as to the basics of Constitutional Law. A district nurse (an over-starched woman with ill-fitting dentures) made a daily call (for what real reason, I have still to determine) and each evening some member of chambers dropped by to keep me up to date with the latest forensic gossip. A monotonous existence, but not too taxing. The lady I employ to keep my flat clean proved herself to be the treasure I'd always suspected her of being; like a genie she appeared each dusk, complete with vacuum flasks and freshly baked bread to break the day's dreary diet of sandwiches (produced by that unimaginative district nurse) with scalding hot, home-made soup, beef stew and a Cockney cheerfulness which turned me into a fitting companion for my evening's visitors.

Nevertheless, a doleful period of my life. But I was not angry. I became angry on that Saturday . . . September the fourteenth.

James propped the crutches against the arm of a chair and said, 'Right. We'll have you out of bed. Gently. Then, we'll adjust them to size.'

'If you seriously think . . .' I exploded.

'Unless, of course, you have visions of being bed-ridden for the rest of your life.'

198

'I can *walk*!' I exploded. 'I use the toilet. I bath . . .'

'That should be a side-splitting spectacle.'

'What?'

'Seeing you in the tub with your left foot stuck in the air.'

'Damn it, man, I can walk.'

'Hobble,' he said.

'All right . . . hobble. But each day . . .'

'I know. You can hobble a little better each day. But that's *all* you'll do. Hobble. Unless you teach those muscles and tendons to *walk* again.'

'With those infernal things,' I sneered.

'You'll bless them before you've finished.'

But I didn't. I never did other than curse them. They gave me freedom of movement; I could leave the flat, visit restaurants, even call in at the chambers. But I still cursed the things. Put a man on crutches and he becomes less than complete. They may be necessary, but they are also humiliating. They are like twin, wooden deformities, stretching from the armpit all the way to the ground: like a third and unwanted leg; like a second, and equally unwanted, head.

'Tuck the tops under your arms . . . as if you're carrying a folded newspaper.'

Thus the advice of James, as I first wobbled around the room on the confounded things.

Fiddlesticks! There is nothing *less* like a folded newspaper. They are awkward, they are heavy and they turn the heads of passing pedestrians. They evoke unwanted – undeserved – sympathy and from men and women who themselves are bent and crippled by a combination of age and diseased joints. They are both an embarrassment and an abomination.

Folded newspapers, indeed!

I tolerated them for little more than a week. On Wednesday, September the twenty-fifth (again, I consult my diary) I threw them aside and substituted

199

two stout walking-sticks. I found the walking-sticks far easier to handle than crutches and, despite James's protestations, I found myself able to *walk* better. Slower, perhaps, but at least I was able (even obliged) to use my legs and feet in a more natural manner.

And each day saw some improvement. By the first week of October I was able to move with reasonable confidence and only using one of the walking-sticks. and on Tuesday, the eighth of October at about four o'clock in the afternoon I strolled into the chambers.

FORTY-THREE

Smith-Hopkinson said, 'I was going to call at your flat this evening.'

'Please do. You're very welcome.'

'With this. It came with the morning post.' He held out an envelope. 'From the size and the postmark I assume it's the same as mine.'

'Indeed.'

I opened the envelope and withdrew an invitation to the wedding of Gerald Patsold and Kathleen Bowling. I was surprised; surprised at the proposed marriage, and surprised that Smith-Hopkinson and I had been invited. I suspect my surprise showed.

'You'll go?' It was part-statement, part-question.

'I really don't know.'

'You met the bride-to-be?'

'Bowling? Yes, the Sunday before the trial. A fine woman.'

'I think we should go,' said Smith-Hopkinson with some finality. 'It's – er – when is it? . . .'

'October twenty-third. A fortnight tomorrow.'

'Wednesday,' he mused. 'Yes, I think we should go.

I've worked very hard these last few weeks. A short break is called for.'

'My apologies,' I grunted. 'Next time, I'll consult the calendar and work-load before I indulge myself in the luxury of an accident.'

'Sorry.' He grinned. 'I think we *should* go,' he added. 'A few deep breaths of Dales air. It might help us survive the coming winter.'

'Possibly.' I still wasn't quite convinced. I argued, 'The obvious drawback. The other guests. They'll be strangers. Empty chatter with people you've never met before – or want to meet again – not a cheerful prospect.'

'Armstrong.'

'And his wife,' I added.

'And of course the happy couple.'

'It's a wedding, for God's sake, not a seminar – they'll be occupied with other things.'

'Y'know . . .' Smith-Hopkinson chewed his lip reflectively. 'It's not impossible. Webb might be there.'

'Webb?' The thought was startling.

'Patsold's friend.'

'Hardly that. He killed Patsold's wife.'

'He's never been charged . . . or, at least, never been tried. I've kept my ear to the ground. Curiosity.'

'It's reputed to be lethal as far as cats are concerned.'

'Oh, come on! You're as interested as *I* am.'

'It's possible,' I admitted grudgingly.

'So . . . let's find out.'

'The chances of Webb being a guest are . . .'

'Armstrong will know.'

'It's finished,' I said. 'We won a case. Not a very difficult case. We didn't make legal history. Dammit, the case should never have been brought. There wasn't enough . . .'

'And yet,' he interrupted teasingly, 'our original plea was going to be Diminished Responsibility. There was *that* much of a case.'

'Are you suggesting . . . ?'

'We won a case,' he soothed. 'Our client was grateful. He's still grateful. Grateful enough to ask us to be guests at his wedding. I think we should accept. Who knows? . . . Webb *might* be there.'

'Rubbish!'

FORTY-FOUR

But he *was*. And such was the strength of his personality that immediately – the moment he strode forward and pumped my hand – he became the same old 'Marty'.

Having accepted the invitation, Smith-Hopkinson and I travelled north on the Tuesday. We booked in at the same Lessford hotel and after breakfast the next morning, we hired a taxi to take us to Pendlebridge. It was a church wedding; a simple affair with less than fifty guests (and that was when I first spotted Marty) and with the reception in an upstairs room of the restaurant where Armstrong and his wife had been my guests at dinner some months before.

The service was uncluttered by externals. There was an organist, but no choir. There was a best man and a maid of honour . . . and that was all. (Momentarily, it struck me as odd that Armstrong hadn't been chosen as best man, but it was none of my business and, anyway, I was not conversant with the degree of friendship between the solicitor and the groom.) Grace, Patsold's partner, wasn't there, but again a wedding did not give medical amnesty to the whole of Pendlebridge, and *somebody* had to be on call to attend the sick and injured. Edward Patsold was there, of course; as pale and as thin as ever, but clean-shaven, decently dressed and with his hair shorn to an acceptable length. From where they sat in the church – and from the manner in which they nodded silent greeting to people unknown to me – I identified Patsold's two daughters, Ruth and Anne.

Everybody else was a stranger and almost before we'd been conducted to a pew by some voluntary usher who had prattled meaningless phrases of welcome, I was regretting having accepted the invitation. Weddings, funerals, christenings . . . they all have the same effect upon me. Even birthdays. Why (I always ask myself) should *I* involve myself in some mock-milestone of some other person's life? Of what importance is that particular day to *me*? It will come, it will pass, with or without either my presence or blessing. Never, since I was born, have I been the 'life and soul' of any party . . . or ever wanted to be. The day of my own birth took place (hopefully) without too much fuss. I have resisted the temptation to marry. My own birthdays come and go quietly and secretly and I receive neither cards nor presents . . . because only *I* know the date. And when I come to the end of my life, my wish is to be disposed of with as little palaver, and as little hypocrisy, as common decency will allow.

I have lived and, during my life, I have done as little harm as possible . . . and that is sufficient reason for existing.

On top of which churches are cold, inhospitable places and, because of an excess of exercise, my heel and ankle hurt more than they'd done for weeks.

Beneath the slow, sonorous organ meanderings, I whispered, 'How long does it last?'

'What?' Smith-Hopkinson talked from the corner of his mouth.

'The service?'

'I don't know. It depends.'

'On what?'

'The hymns. The parson . . . I suppose.'

'Ye gods!' I groaned.

'What?'

'I have yet to meet a cleric who wasn't madly in love with his own voice.'

I felt the pew move slightly as Smith-Hopkinson tried to control a chuckle.

'I have no intentions of kneeling,' I muttered.

'One of the seven deadly sins . . . don't forget that.'

'What is?'

'Pride.'

'Pride be damned. This foot of mine is particularly painful.'

'Hush.' Smith-Hopkinson touched my knee. 'Here she comes.'

On cue the organist slipped smoothly into *Here Comes the Bride*, and every neck twisted to see the entrance of Kate Bowling. And (the truth must be told) her appearance verified the impression I'd had at the meeting arranged by Armstrong. A woman tempered – but at the same time in some strange way mellowed – by the hardships of her life. A proud woman who held herself well; who did nothing to hide her middle years, but who was quietly conscious of a natural, basic beauty. A strong woman, but not a hard woman. Her step was as gently firm as ever, and the presence of the elderly man at her side was quite unnecessary.

She wore a tailored two-piece in dark blue with white pipings. Her matching blue hat was wide-brimmed; but not wide-brimmed enough to make it look even faintly ridiculous. In her white-gloved hands she held a single, fern-framed orchid.

Smith-Hopkinson murmured, 'He has taste.'

'*She* has taste,' I corrected him softly. 'What *he* has is good fortune.'

The service? The normal mixtures of wilt-thou and I-will; the old fashioned wording, which included a promise to obey. I kept *my* promise; I did not kneel,

204

but at the appropriate moments I bowed my head on to hands clasped over the curve of my walking-stick. (I argued that, if there was an Almighty, and assuming he was interested in my bodily contortions, he must have been aware of the pain in my foot and, if he wasn't prepared to make some small allowance for *that* then, on the basis of some of my past escapades, I was already well beyond hope . . . so why kneel?)

By 2.30 pm we were shuffling from the church and easing ourselves into a shuttle-service of cars to the restaurant.

It was a cold, help-yourself buffet, but excellent. With everything from smoked salmon to ice-cream – from a gateaux selection calculated to test young stomachs to the point of destruction, to an equally varied selection of savouries for the less adventurous digestive systems – all neatly arranged atop starched table-linen in a display which stretched along three sides of the large room. And booze. One could have a modest beer and from there move all the way through the exotica of grain and grape to the peak of top-quality champagne.

As we entered the room Smith-Hopkinson murmured, 'My word!'

I glanced at him and noted that the exclamation related both to the food *and* to an unescorted female charmer who had obviously arrived only minutes before us. On the theory that youth, even in the confined world of the Inns of Court, must occasionally have its fling, I excused myself, found a plate and, with venison pâté sandwiches and watered-down whisky, settled myself into one of the scattering of armchairs.

The crowd thickened, there were the usual speeches, punctuated by the usual guffaws at non-jokes, then the newly-weds left for a honeymoon somewhere . . . and the guests set about the task of eating and drinking themselves into a state of stupor.

Armstrong and his wife approached me.

I made to rise from the armchair, but Ruth Armstrong smiled and said, 'Please don't. We've been watching you. You've obviously hurt your left leg.'

'Left foot,' I corrected her. 'The truth is I shouldn't be allowed within a hundred yards of a paint brush.'

'Nice to see you, sir,' said Armstrong.

'Thank you.' I turned my head, looked at his wife and said, 'She's as pretty as ever. I hope you still appreciate that fact.'

'I do. Indeed, I do.'

Armstrong pulled two high-backed chairs nearer, they sat down and we indulged in friendly, but not too serious, small talk.

Then, because my curiosity got the better of me, I said, 'I spotted Webb in the congregation.'

'Yes.' Armstrong seemed to bite the word off.

'Lack of evidence?' I asked gently.

'Too much evidence.'

'Darling.' His wife's tone held a pleading quality.

'He should know,' said Armstrong harshly.

'Know what?' I asked.

'He was as guilty as hell.'

'Patsold?'

'As guilty as hell,' he repeated.

'I find that a little difficult to . . .'

'It *can* be done.'

'Darling,' repeated Ruth Armstrong. 'I thought we'd . . .'

'Yes.' He nodded, heavily. 'We've had it all out. It's water under the bridge . . . that's why we're here. But they know. *Everybody* knows. That makes *me* suspect. A shyster. That makes people . . .'

'*I* don't know,' I interrupted. 'Perhaps I should.'

He glanced at his wife, and she smiled a resigned smile and sighed a resigned sigh.

He rose to his feet and said, 'My office. It's in the next street. It shouldn't take more than half an hour.'

FORTY-FIVE

My name is Gerald Patsold. I am a medical practitioner in the township of Pendlebridge. On Monday and Tuesday, July the first and second of this year, I was tried at Lessford Crown Court, charged with the murder of my wife, Elizabeth Patsold. I was acquitted. I now wish it to be known that that verdict was an incorrect verdict. I was, and still am, guilty of the murder of my wife via manual strangulation. On the evening of Tuesday, May the seventh I learned from my friend Martin Webb of the condition of my wife. That she was pregnant. That he, Martin Webb, was the possible father of the unborn child. That he, Martin Webb, had been having an affair with my wife for some time. I was aware that I could not possibly be the man responsible for my wife's condition. I had undergone a successful vasectomy operation, six years previously. I was not surprised at the information given to me by Martin Webb. I had strongly suspected unfaithfulness, on the part of my wife, for a number of years. I was not angry with Martin Webb. I valued his friendship, and still value his friendship, above any show of empty jealousy based upon a marriage which, by this time, had come to have no real meaning. The information of my wife's condition was given to me, by Martin Webb, while we were both in the consulting room of my surgery. I left that surgery alone, went home and confronted my wife with what I had learned. She made no denial. She taunted me. An argument, then a fight, ensued. During the fight, my wife clawed my face. I strangled her to death. I did this quite deliberately, knowing full well what I was doing. When she was dead, I sat in an armchair. My son, Edward returned home, saw his dead mother and saw me. I pretended not to be aware of his presence. Edward telephoned the police and, throughout police questioning, I continued the pretence that I could not remember having killed my wife. At my trial, and upon the advice of my solicitor, Reginald Armstrong, I pleaded Not Guilty to the charge. I was defended by Mr Simon Whitehouse, Q.C. Whitehouse was recommended to me by Martin Webb. I realise there has been a miscarriage of justice, and that I should have been convicted of the murder of my wife. I do not wish any other person to stand accused of committing a murder committed by me. I was quite sane when I strangled my wife. I knew exactly what I was doing. I was assisted by nobody. I am in full possession of my senses at this moment, and know exactly what I am doing. My intention is to sign and date this document in the presence of my solicitor, Reginald Armstrong, and to ask him to witness and date my signature.

The confession was signed 'G. Patsold', witnessed by 'R. Armstrong' and dated July the third . . . the day after Patsold's acquittal.

It was a photostat copy and I dropped it on to Armstrong's desk and waited.

'The original's with the police,' he said in a low voice. 'I don't have to tell you what *they* think.'

'And you?' I asked.

'What?'

'What do *you* think?'

'I think it's a con. Made to get Webb off the hook.'

'He's safe, of course. Patsold, I mean.'

'Of course. The Double Jeopardy rule makes it impossible for him to be charged with the same murder twice. And by this "confession" – so-called – it's virtually impossible to hang a charge around Webb's neck.'

'You witnessed the signature,' I reminded him.

'I was a mug.' The self-disgust was plain to see. 'To

"put his house in order" ... that's what he said. Just witness his signature. Hell ... I trusted the man. I was his *friend*.'

'You didn't read it?'

'No. "Very personal", again his own words.'

'You are,' I said gently, 'a very foolish young man.'

'Gullible. But not any more. Ever!'

'And Webb?'

'He's in it.' He moved his hands in a gesture of helplessness. 'He *has* to be in it. He knows about the law ... the law relating to insanity.'

'Most people know the basics.'

'More than the basics. Remember the trial? His evidence? He *explained* that law to the jury. *Mens rea* ... the lot. The Tolson decision. Even Belmont couldn't fault him. The summing up – the part relating to *mens rea* – was built upon what Webb had already said.'

Armstrong was a young man with a chip on his shoulder. A very large chip. And in fairness, who could blame him. His name had been mentioned in the 'confession'; he'd even witnessed the signature. Come to that, *my* name was also included, albeit without the same possible implication. A solicitor. His duty was to advise a client. But (before that) his duty was to learn the truth . . . and, thereafter, base his advice upon that truth. Read that 'confession' with a biased mind, and certain unsavoury conclusions might be reached. Conclusions which the Law Society would frown upon.

Armstrong had cause for his concern.

'The copy?' I nodded at the photostat.

'From Leroy. He has the original.'

'On file?'

'It's already been to the D.P.P. Complete with a transcript of the trial and depositions. Returned "No Action" ... insufficient evidence.'

'Obviously.'

'But insufficient evidence against *whom*? Look . . .'
He leaned forward in the desk chair. 'This is a tight
little community. Pendlebridge. Whispers. Rumours.
There's been a slight leak. Deliberately? Accidentally? I
don't know. Who ever *does* know? But gradually it's
getting me a name. A name I can do without.'
'The confidence of the local courts,' I murmured.
'I'm losing it . . . fast.'
We sat in silence for a few minutes, and I allowed my
gaze to wander around the office. A good office; the
office of a successful young solicitor; free of all mustiness; shelved along two walls with books covering all
aspects of the Law. I could imagine, without difficulty,
the high esteem in which he'd been held locally. With
equal ease I could also imagine the withdrawal of that
esteem in a place like Pendlebridge should any whisper
of 'shysterism' come to the ear of the locals. These
people were not 'smart'. They used the law . . . they
didn't abuse it. Armstrong had a fight on his hands.
'Conspiracy?' I suggested. 'Patsold and Webb?'
'We're blocked,' he said sadly. 'Don't think I haven't
spent hours thinking out all the angles. Conspiracy to
murder. But Patsold's innocent . . . in law. Whatever
this "confession" says. The final crime – murder – was
completed. But, technically, *not* by Patsold. And you
must have two or more for Conspiracy to hold water.
Patsold's innocent . . . Webb isn't even *allowed* to be
guilty.'
'To Pervert the Course of Justice?'
'No way.' He shook his head. 'Patsold stood trial . . .
he *could* have been convicted. This damn "confession".
An attempt by him to *ensure* justice . . . should the
wrong man be charged.'
'Coming and going,' I murmured.
'Left, right and sideways,' he agreed.
'So?' I held my head on one side. 'Why attend his
wedding?'

'I heard you might be here.'

'And?'

'I need help,' he said simply.

'You know the law. As well as – better than – I do.'

'*You* know Webb.'

'Well enough,' I agreed. 'Perhaps *too* well.'

'Y'mean, he can't be got at?'

'I'm an old man,' I said solemnly. 'Webb – he's the same age – but he's stayed young.'

'I'm sorry.' He stood up from the desk chair.

'I'll talk to him,' I promised.

'That's all I ask.'

FORTY-SIX

Armstrong and I returned to the reception and, by that time, the chairs had been pushed to the wall, a record-player was throbbing out 'pop' and the younger members of the wedding guests were indulging themselves in that ritualistic shuffling which these days masquerades under the name of 'dancing'. Armstrong located his wife, we shook hands, and they left. I limped around the perimeter of the dance-space, found the table from which drinks were being dispensed and ended up with a triple whisky in a tumbler glass topped to the brim with iced water. It was what I needed; something to cushion the realisation that both Armstrong and I had been made to look a little foolish.

Then as I sipped my drink and indulged in a brown study of mild self-pity that voice – that undeniably magnificent voice – burst in on my thoughts.

'Simon, old son. I've been looking for you since I spotted you in church. Where the devil have you been hiding yourself?'

I turned and Marty was there, with a great friendly

smile on his face, and his hand held out in greeting. Automatically – with all the non-will of a Pavlovian dog – I placed my drink on the table, grasped the proffered hand and he pumped away and momentarily he was the same old 'Marty'. I even managed a watery smile.

He jerked his head and said, 'Not our music?'

'If it can be called "music".'

'Indeed.' He chuckled. 'Your colleague seems to be enjoying himself.'

'Smith-Hopkinson?' I looked past Marty's frame and saw that young man moving, in more-or-less strict tempo, with one of the more delightful ladies held in his arms. I said, 'A young man and unattached gentleman. At his age . . .' I left the sentence unfinished.

'We were just as randy.' Marty ended the sentence for me.

'One of us,' I agreed.

'But today not our world.'

'Not *my* world, Marty. Not – what's the present ridiculous expression? – not my "bag".'

'You think I'm different?'

'Less musty.' I tasted my drink. 'We agreed upon that when last I came north . . . remember?'

'Can I ever forget?' The smile looked genuine enough; It was, moreover, a smile without rancour . . . if it *was* genuine. It expanded into a grin and he said, 'You can still fight, Simon. I knew you could. I was depending on it.'

'With such a knowledge of the mind,' I murmured. 'Who needs a crystal ball?'

'Armstrong?'

'He's not a happy man.'

'He's young. He'll recover.'

'Age . . . again.' I mocked him a little. 'Your phobia, Marty. Even *you*. Your weakness. Your hidden fear. That you're getting old . . . past it.'

212

'I could prove you wrong.'

'Aah!'

'Your foot.' He seemed, suddenly, to notice my walking-stick. 'You've hurt your foot.'

'I, too, forgot my age.'

'A break?'

'Of a sort.'

'Let's find somewhere to sit,' he suggested. 'Sit . . . and talk.'

'Not here. Not with this noise.'

'There's a room along the corridor. One of those lecture rooms places like this for hire occasionally.'

'Are you going to lecture me?' I asked gently.

'Each other . . . perhaps.' He picked up an unopened bottle of whisky and a clean tumbler. 'We could get drunk while we're doing it. Like old times.'

'That,' I said solemnly, 'would be very civilised.'

'Wouldn't it, though?'

'But – to be *really* civilised – with soda.'

'Of course.' He hooked a finger inside the empty tumbler and picked up a siphon of soda. He held out an arm and said, 'After you, Simon. What is it? . . . age before beauty.'

'Shall we say "The bishop before the curate".'

He laughed, lowered his arm and allowed me to pass. We left the reception room and, as the swing-doors closed behind us, the noise – and the happiness – died. We strolled along a short corridor and he opened a door on the right; a door leading to a small, intimate room with rows of folding chairs, a small platform and, on the platform, a blackboard and easel. The curved chalk-marks and the scribbled words on the blackboard suggested that the room had last been used by a class interested in flower arrangement. We settled on two of the chairs in the front row, using a third chair as a makeshift table. He unscrewed the top from the whisky bottle, poured himself rather more whisky than I'd

213

taken in my own tumbler, then added a liberal squirt of soda.

He raised the glass, smiled, and said, 'Here's to old friendships.'

'To old friendships.' I raised my own glass, and we each drank to whatever we meant.

Teasingly I said, 'What was she like, Marty?'

'Beth?'

'Elizabeth Patsold. Was she *really* worth a ruined career?'

'No.' He shook his head and tasted his drink. 'None of them are, old son. But on the other hand, she didn't ruin a career.'

'She can't have helped yours.'

'Not the old world, Simon. Not the world in which *we* learned our respective trades. The great god . . . permissiveness. That's the name of the present game.'

'Nevertheless . . .'

'It's no longer remembered.' And from the tone of his voice, I knew he was speaking the truth. 'The police? They tend to bear a grudge, perhaps. But they're helpless. The rest?' His lips bent into a smile. 'If anything, it's enhanced my reputation at the university.'

'Practical psychology,' I murmured.

'That . . . and other things.'

'You've let it be known, of course?'

'Quietly,' he admitted. 'A hint here, a hint there. To keep perfection under cover . . . a crime, surely?'

'Perfection?'

'To use the law, as a means of defeating the law.'

'*Mens rea* . . . and all that.'

He smiled, tipped some of his drink down his throat, and said, '*Mens rea*. Double Jeopardy. Conspiracy. Reasonable doubt. I think we covered everything.'

'We?'

'Patsold went along.'

'But the brains – the *real* planning – you of course?'

And if *he* knew men, *I* knew Marty. I needed the whole story; every sordid, every trifling, detail. Part of it was pure curiosity, part of it was some wild possibility that he'd left some tiny breach in his defences. Law was my life – in effect, it was my love and the only love I'd ever known – and this man had taken my law (my love) and sullied it. Which to me made my love of the law as empty and as self-delusory as had been my supposed 'love' of Alice Pearson. The few things (the very few things) which had ever aroused emotion in me . . . and this man ravished them without a second thought. I was (perhaps always had been) his plaything.

But I knew Marty; I knew the size of his monumental ego; I knew the subtle cruelties he enjoyed . . . and I played upon them. Therefore we sat in that deserted lecture room and, as we gradually consumed a whole bottle of whisky, I eased open *his* mind. And he told me . . . everything.

Patsold had attended his lectures and, because Patsold had become so interested in psychology and psychiatry, a friendship had developed. But (as always with Marty) friendship, in the shape of innocent companionship, was not enough. He visited Patsold's home, met Patsold's wife and in her saw one more sexual conquest.

'. . . You get to know the signs, Simon. The look in the eye. The choice of phrase. The way they're so damned *demure*.' He tipped more whisky down his throat. 'The teasers don't function that way, old son. Take my word. They're brash. Blatant. Embarrassingly so. But the real whores? You can hold a conversation with 'em in a secret language. A roomful of people . . . it doesn't matter. You're taking about "it". You know. She knows. Nobody else even guesses . . .'

But (or so it seemed) Marty 'guessed' and was right. The cuckolded Patsold was too busy – perhaps too tired – to perform his husbandly duties and his wife sought solace elsewhere. And (but naturally!) Marty obliged.

'... Didn't you feel guilty?'

'Guilty? Why the devil should I feel guilty? I wasn't raping the woman. Looked at objectively, it can be argued I was doing the man a favour.'

'The argument escapes me.'

'My dear old Simon. Think who she *might* have been romping around with ...'

And of course (nature being inclined that way) Elizabeth Patsold became pregnant. She explained the impossibility of her husband being the father. She even suggested marriage.

'... She was raving mad, of course.'

'By that you mean she didn't appreciate the immorality of the old lecher she'd become involved with.'

'I'm not the marrying kind, Simon.'

'But her husband had to be told?'

'Of course ...'

And he was told. By Marty. And (Marty being Marty) the telling thereof was done smoothly, and without any real interference between the friendship of the two men. I would like to have been present at that conversation, even by the high standards of Martin Webb, it must have been a *tour de force*.

'... Actually he wasn't too surprised.'

'Really?'

'Well, if somewhat surprised . . . not unduly outraged.'

'Indeed?'

'Kate, you see.'

'Kathleen Bowling?'

'You've seen her. Quite a cut above the average female.'

'Handsome.'

'Indeed . . . far more handsome than his wife. And – to coin a phrase – eager ...'

216

The situation, then. A licentious Marty, being annoyed by a mistress who had thoughtlessly become pregnant. The husband of that mistress – still Marty's friend – who, in turn, entertained amorous feelings towards another woman, who in turn, reciprocated those feelings.

Murder and sex. The two things were ever intertwined. At a guess they always will be. Murder, you see, while tending to be slightly messy, and not a little dangerous, is quicker, cheaper and far more final than either divorce or separation. There is no *decree nisi* in murder . . . only decree absolute.

There was a moment – there *must* have been a moment – when by mutual (albeit) unspoken agreement the life of the unfortunate Elizabeth Patsold had only a limited time to run.

'. . . Your idea, of course.'

'The finer details.'

'Patsold took a risk.'

'Not really. At least, *he* didn't think he did.'

'He could have been convicted.'

'Not with the right barrister. A solicitor who believed him to be innocent. Some carefully planted "evidence" . . . planted where the Defence *would* find it, but the police *wouldn't*.'

'They might have searched the surgery.'

'They might, indeed.'

'And?'

'The capsule would have been "lost" somewhere else. Somewhere the police *hadn't* searched.'

'I don't follow.'

'Duplicate keys, old son. I had the full set . . . made before Patsold gave his performance. Anywhere. Where *he* could go, *I* could go. And – a few discreet enquiries – I soon learned where the police *hadn't* been.'

'That's clever. One might say perfect.'

217

'I think so. As with the choice of barrister. Armstrong virtually chose himself. *I* chose you.'

'Should I feel honoured?'

'I think so. A man known to be so thorough. To be so *reliable*...'

The fact is, I didn't feel honoured. I felt very *dishonoured*. Marty's yardstick of 'reliability' – his opinion of my 'thoroughness' – gave me no cause for pride. 'Gullibility' rather than 'reliability' seemed the right word. But I hid my outrage, and continued to tease the truth from him.

By this time, the whisky had loosened his tongue a little. He was tending to brag. To over-enthuse. Perhaps even to gild the gingerbread.

As he told the story, Patsold was little more than a slow-witted dolt; a man who had to be guided carefully along each path; an amateur, needing endless rehearsal before he could play his part to perfection.

'... Just to kill the woman, then sit down and look stupid.'

'To murder his wife?'

'Of course.'

'To strangle her? Manually?'

'Naturally.'

'There's nothing "natural" about it, Marty. He had the difficult role to play.'

'Damned if he had.'

'Or at the very least the most dangerous.'

'Just to kill the infernal woman. After that to keep his mouth shut and his mind closed. That's neither difficult nor dangerous.'

'And you?'

'I had *you* to deal with, old son. Not some dim-witted copper. Oh, no. My task was infinitely more difficult. A Q.C., no less, and *I* had to feed him *sub judice* hints without frightening him away, and without letting him spot the bait...'

After that it was easy; easy, that is, as Marty told it.
The more I dug, the more I found, the more I found,
the stronger the Defence, the stronger the Defence, the
more certain of an acquittal, the more certain of an
acquittal, the safer for all concerned. To use the law
to *defeat* the law. To take three established legal
presumptions – plus, of course, a certain amount of
play-acting, plus the careful planting of evidence for
the Defence, plus (again of course) a defending barrister whose contorted memory of an episode in his
student days clouded any real objectivity – and, from
this carefully measured concoction, create a situation
in which murder could be committed, if not with im-
punity, at least with reasonable safety . . . and, moreover,
to be in a position where it was possible to boast of this
'home run' through the forensic obstacles.

We were nearing the end of our session. The whisky
bottle was almost empty. For myself (thanks, perhaps,
to the intake of liquid good spirit) I could feel very
little anger. A certain amount of admiration, perhaps;
after all, it isn't every day one is privileged to hear a
blow-by-blow account of the perfect murder.

And, of course, Marty was becoming insufferably
self-satisfied.

'. . . You legal eagles. You'll have to do some re-
thinking.'

'Because of this drug?'

'Dimethyltryptamine? There are others, old son.
Quite a few. New ones every year.'

'And – correct me, if I'm wrong – they turn an ordinary, decent man (or woman) into a homicidal maniac?'

'More or less. They screw up the chemistry of the
brain . . . that's what it boils down to.'

'Madness.'

'That's a very emotive word.' He hiccuped gently.
'Pardon. Who isn't mad, old boy? Who isn't slightly
round the bend? Those nincompoops in the other room,

219

suffering what they call "music". *They're* mad ... by our standards. But they think *we're* mad ... because we enjoy the traditional stuff. *You're* mad, old son, for having so much faith in your beloved law. Everybody's mad about something.'

'And you're mad about synthetic drugs, right?'

'Right.' He nodded with all the solemnity of a drunken man. 'Mad enough,' I said, 'to take DMT from a hospital dispensary. Against your own signature. Then not being able to account for it.'

'I lost it.' He grinned.

'The hell you lost it. You hid it in a Lentizol capsule.'

'I didn't hide it, Simon, old friend. I didn't *hide* it. Some of the patients on the ward. They take Lentizol, see? So, when necessary we slip that something extra into the Lentizol capsule and they don't object. They don't know, so they don't object.'

'DMT, for example?'

'If necessary. It saves a lot of arguing. Sometimes – y'know – they get *very* awkward, *very* suspicious, if they think we're trying something new. That's all. That's what the DMT was doing in the Lentizol capsule. All five microgrammes, old son. You identified it. What you didn't do was *measure* it ... thank God. If you'd *measured* it ...'

'Patsold would have gone to prison.'

'I suppose. Yes ... I suppose.'

'And you?'

'My dear old Simon. All *I* did was misplace a doctored Lentizol capsule. Very remiss, of course.'

'Remiss?'

'That's what they said.' I think it was meant to be a chuckle but, because of the whisky, it sounded more like a schoolgirl's giggle. 'The hospital authority. Very cross with me, but relieved, of course, when they read a copy of Patsold's statement. That it had all been a

220

put-on. Not the result of taking DMT, after all. *And all the DMT was recovered.* A bit of a caution. "Don't do it again." I promised not to. But – y'know – *very* remiss of me to misplace a dangerous drug like that. A good job you found it, old boy. Otherwise I'd have been in *real* trouble ...'

FORTY-SEVEN

'We have,' mused Smith-Hopkinson, 'been taken to the cleaners.'
'In the vernacular,' I agreed.
It was the Thursday – the day after the wedding – and we were travelling south in the Pullman from Harrogate. We'd lunched and were sipping wine (surprisingly good wine) and I'd thought it only fair to explain to my colleague the details of the fiasco which, in the court records, was itemised as R. *v.* Patsold. I'd missed nothing out; no ploy, no argument, no carefully constructed blind alley. It was, if nothing else, an object lesson in how *not* to approach a Defence brief.
Outside the October afternoon did little to cheer us. We'd passed Grantham and, as the carriage swayed slightly, it seemed almost as if the dull greyness of the day was pressing down on the speeding train in a futile attempt to impede its progress.
'He'll get away with it?' Smith-Hopkinson made it a question; a question shot with mild surprise.
'Webb?'
'Not – er – "Marty" anymore?'
'Webb,' I repeated grimly.
'But he *will* get away with it?'
'He's already *got* away with it ... wouldn't you say?'
'A pity.'

221

'I will,' I promised, 'let Belmont know. Officially, but not publicly. Judges . . . they can sometimes do things.'

'Belmont won't like it.'

'I'm counting on him positively *hating* it.'

'And?'

'The Home Secretary. The D.P.P. The hospital service and the law . . . they converge in that rarefied atmosphere. Something *must* be done.'

'For instance?'

'My dear boy, I'm only a struggling barrister. The Powers-that-Be . . . they'll find some rear door through which they can evict Webb.'

'Hopefully.'

'Hopefully,' I agreed.

We were silent for a few moments, then Smith-Hopkinson murmured, 'Investigative journalism.'

'A subject I know little about.'

'I have friends.' Smith-Hopkinson offered me a cigarette, but I declined. He lit his own, then holding the cigarette between his fingers, he seemed to mouth his thoughts gently at the smouldering tip. He said, 'Webb. He's surrounded by enemies. Armstrong on one side. Belmont – plus the heavyweight officialdom – on the other. Patsold? If Patsold talks, Webb's in queer street. If Webb says too much . . . *Patsold's* equally at risk. Men have to trust each other a great deal in that sort of situation. Enough pressure . . . public opinion just *might* force a re-trial.'

'In law there's no . . .'

'The law can be changed. Who knows? Investigative journalism. It brought down a president. And *he* tried to hide behind the law.'

'Your friends?' I asked quietly.

'They'll dig. All they need is a gimmick. Something to start the ball rolling.'

'We can't do that. I'm sorry, but . . .'

'Not us.' He smiled gently. 'The sanctity of the Bar.

222

I know. But the new Mrs Patsold. *She's* the way in. Two husbands. The first killed their child. The second killed his first wife. That's a gimmick . . . all they need. Why? Why does she *always* end up with a man charged with murder? That's worth headlines, then they take it from there?'

'I wonder,' I breathed.

'They'll topple,' he promised gravely. 'A year, two years, enough questions, enough publicity, enough pressure. They'll topple.'

I leaned back in my seat, stared from the window at the grey landscape and (in my own way) I prayed.